A Romance of Yo

by

Francois Coppee

With a Preface by JOSE DE HEREDIA, of the French Academy

The Echo Library 2007

Published by

The Echo Library

Echo Library
131 High St.
Teddington
Middlesex TW11 8HH

www.echo-library.com

Please report serious faults in the text to complaints@echo-library.com

ISBN 978-1-40684-864-9

FRANCOIS COPPEE

FRANCOIS EDOUARD JOACHIM COPPEE was born in Paris, January 12, 1842. His father was a minor 'employe' in the French War Office; and, as the family consisted of six the parents, three daughters, and a son (the subject of this essay)—the early years of the poet were not spent in great luxury. After the father's death, the young man himself entered the governmental office with its monotonous work. In the evening he studied hard at St. Genevieve Library. He made rhymes, had them even printed (Le Reliquaire, 1866); but the public remained indifferent until 1869, when his comedy in verse, 'Le Passant', appeared. From this period dates the reputation of Coppee—he woke up one morning a "celebrated man."

Like many of his countrymen, he is a poet, a dramatist, a novelist, and a writer of fiction. He was elected to the French Academy in 1884. Smooth shaven, of placid figure, with pensive eyes, the hair brushed back regularly, the head of an artist, Coppee can be seen any day looking over the display of the Parisian secondhand booksellers on the Quai Malaquais; at home on the writing-desk, a page of carefully prepared manuscript, yet sometimes covered by cigarette-ashes; upon the wall, sketches by Jules Lefebvre and Jules Breton; a little in the distance, the gaunt form of his attentive sister and companion, Annette, occupied with household cares, ever fearful of disturbing him. Within this tranquil domicile can be heard the noise of the Parisian faubourg with its thousand different dins; the bustle of the street; the clatter of a factory; the voice of the workshop; the cries of the pedlers intermingled with the chimes of the bells of a near-by convent-a confusing buzzing noise, which the author, however, seems to enjoy; for Coppee is Parisian by birth, Parisian by education, a Parisian of the Parisians.

If as a poet we contemplate him, Coppee belongs to the group commonly called "Parnassiens"—not the Romantic School, the sentimental lyric effusion of Lamartine, Hugo, or De Musset! When the poetical lute was laid aside by the triad of 1830, it was taken up by men of quite different stamp, of even opposed tendencies. Observation of exterior matters was now greatly adhered to in poetry; it became especially descriptive and scientific; the aim of every poet was now to render most exactly, even minutely, the impressions received, or faithfully to translate into artistic language a thesis of philosophy, a discovery of science. With such a poetical doctrine, you will easily understand the importance which the "naturalistic form" henceforth assumed.

Coppee, however, is not only a maker of verses, he is an artist and a poet. Every poem seems to have sprung from a genuine inspiration. When he sings, it is because he has something to sing about, and the result is that his poetry is nearly always interesting. Moreover, he respects the limits of his art; for while his friend and contemporary, M. Sully-Prudhomme, goes astray habitually into philosophical speculation, and his immortal senior, Victor Hugo, often declaims, if one may venture to say so, in a manner which is tedious, Coppee sticks rigorously to what may be called the proper regions of poetry.

Francois Coppee is not one of those superb high priests disdainful of the throng: he is the poet of the "humble," and in his work, 'Les Humbles', he paints with a sincere emotion his profound sympathy for the sorrows, the miseries, and the sacrifices of the meek. Again, in his 'Grave des Forgerons, Le Naufrage, and L'Epave', all poems of great extension and universal reputation, he treats of simple existences, of unknown unfortunates, and of sacrifices which the daily papers do not record. The coloring and designing are precise, even if the tone be somewhat sombre, and nobody will deny that Coppee most fully possesses the technique of French poetry.

But Francois Coppee is known to fame as a prosewriter, too. His 'Contes en prose' and his 'Vingt Contes Nouveaux' are gracefully and artistically told; scarcely one of the 'contes' fails to have a moral motive. The stories are short and naturally slight; some, indeed, incline rather to the essay than to the story, but each has that enthralling interest which justifies its existence. Coppee possesses preeminently the gift of presenting concrete fact rather than abstraction. A sketch, for instance, is the first tale written by him, 'Une Idylle pendant le Seige' (1875). In a novel we require strong characterization, great grasp of character, and the novelist should show us the human heart and intellect in full play and activity. In 1875 appeared also 'Olivier', followed by 'L'Exilee (1876); Recits et Elegies (1878); Vingt Contes Nouveaux (1883); and Toute une Jeunesse', mainly an autobiography, crowned by acclaim by the Academy. 'Le Coupable' was published in 1897. Finally, in 1898, appeared 'La Bonne Souffrance'. In the last-mentioned work it would seem that the poet, just recovering from a severe malady, has returned to the dogmas of the Catholic Church, wherefrom he, like so many of his contemporaries, had become estranged when a youth. The poems of 1902, 'Dans la Priere et dans la Lutte', tend to confirm the correctness of this view.

Thanks to the juvenile Sarah Bernhardt, Coppee became, as before mentioned, like Byron, celebrated in one night. This happened through the performance of 'Le Passant'.

As interludes to the plays there are "occasional" theatrical pieces, written for the fiftieth anniversary of the performance of 'Hernani' or the two-hundredth anniversary of the foundation of the "Comedie Francaise." This is a wide field, indeed, which M. Coppee has cultivated to various purposes.

Take Coppee's works in their sum and totality, and the world-decree is that he is an artist, and an admirable one. He plays upon his instrument with all power and grace. But he is no mere virtuoso. There is something in him beyond the executant. Of Malibran, Alfred de Musset says, most beautifully, that she had that "voice of the heart which alone has power to reach the heart." Here, also, behind the skilful player on language, the deft manipulator of rhyme and rhythm, the graceful and earnest writer, one feels the beating of a human heart. One feels that he is giving us personal impressions of life and its joys and sorrows; that his imagination is powerful because it is genuinely his own; that the flowers of his fancy spring spontaneously from the soil. Nor can I regard it as aught but an added grace that the strings of his instrument should vibrate so readily to what is beautiful and unselfish and delicate in human feeling.

JOSE DE HEREDIA

de l'Academie Francaise.

A ROMANCE OF YOUTH

BOOK 1.

CHAPTER I

ON THE BALCONY

As far back as Amedee Violette can remember, he sees himself in an infant's cap upon a fifth-floor balcony covered with convolvulus; the child was very small, and the balcony seemed very large to him. Amedee had received for a birthday present a box of water-colors, with which he was sprawled out upon an old rug, earnestly intent upon his work of coloring the woodcuts in an odd volume of the 'Magasin Pittoresque', and wetting his brush from time to time in his mouth. The neighbors in the next apartment had a right to one-half of the balcony. Some one in there was playing upon the piano Marcailhou's Indiana Waltz, which was all the rage at that time. Any man, born about the year 1845, who does not feel the tears of homesickness rise to his eyes as he turns over the pages of an old number of the 'Magasin Pittoresque', or who hears some one play upon an old piano Marcailhou's Indiana Waltz, is not endowed with much sensibility.

When the child was tired of putting the "flesh color" upon the faces of all the persons in the engravings, he got up and went to peep through the railings of the balustrade. He saw extending before him, from right to left, with a graceful curve, the Rue Notre-Dame-des-Champs, one of the quietest streets in the Luxembourg quarter, then only half built up. The branches of the trees spread over the wooden fences, which enclosed gardens so silent and tranquil that passers by could hear the birds singing in their cages.

It was a September afternoon, with a broad expanse of pure sky across which large clouds, like mountains of silver, moved in majestic slowness.

Suddenly a soft voice called him:

"Amedee, your father will return from the office soon. We must wash your hands before we sit down to the table, my darling."

His mother came out upon the balcony for him. His mother; his dear mother, whom he knew for so short a time! It needs an effort for him to call her to mind now, his memories are so indistinct. She was so modest and pretty, so pale, and with such charming blue eyes, always carrying her head on one side, as if the weight of her lovely chestnut hair was too heavy for her to bear, and smiling the sweet, tired smile of those who have not long to live! She made his toilette, kissed him upon his forehead, after brushing his hair. Then she laid their modest table, which was always decorated with a pretty vase of flowers. Soon the father entered. He was one of those mild, unpretentious men who let everybody run over them.

He tried to be gay when he entered his own house. He raised his little boy aloft with one arm, before kissing him, exclaiming, "Houp la!" A moment later he kissed his young wife and held her close to him, tenderly, as he asked, with an anxious look:

"Have you coughed much to-day?"

She always replied, hanging her head like a child who tells an untruth, "No, not very much."

The father would then put on an old coat—the one he took off was not very new. Amedee was then seated in a high chair before his mug, and the young mother, going into the kitchen, would bring in the supper. After opening his napkin, the father would brush back behind his ear with his hand a long lock on the right side, that always fell into his eyes.

"Is there too much of a breeze this evening? you afraid to go out upon the balcony, Lucie? Put a shawl on, then," said M. Violette, while his wife was pouring the water remaining in the carafe upon a box where some nasturtiums were growing.

"No, Paul, I am sure—take Amedee down from his chair, and let us go out upon the balcony."

It was cool upon this high balcony. The sun had set, and now the great clouds resembled mountains of gold, and a fresh odor came up from the surrounding gardens.

"Good-evening, Monsieur Violette," suddenly said a cordial voice. "What a fine evening!"

It was their neighbor, M. Gerard, an engraver, who had also come to take breath upon his end of the balcony, having spent the entire day bent over his work. He was large and bald-headed, with a good-natured face, a red beard sprinkled with white hairs, and he wore a short, loose coat. As he spoke he lighted his clay pipe, the bowl of which represented Abd-el-Kader's face, very much colored, save the eyes and turban, which were of white enamel.

The engraver's wife, a dumpy little woman with merry eyes, soon joined her husband, pushing before her two little girls; one, the smaller of the two, was two years younger than Amedee; the other was ten years old, and already had a wise little air. She was the pianist who practised one hour a day Marcailhou's Indiana Waltz.

The children chattered through the trellis that divided the balcony in two parts. Louise, the elder of the girls, knew how to read, and told the two little ones very beautiful stories: Joseph sold by his brethren; Robinson Crusoe discovering the footprints of human beings.

Amedee, who now has gray hair upon his temples, can still remember the chills that ran down his back at the moment when the wolf, hidden under coverings and the grandmother's cap, said, with a gnashing of teeth, to little Red Riding Hood: "All the better to eat you with, my child."

It was almost dark then upon the terrace. It was all delightfully terrible!

During this time the two families, in their respective parts of the balcony, were talking familiarly together. The Violettes were quiet people, and preferred rather to listen to their neighbors than to talk themselves, making brief replies for politeness' sake—"Ah!" "Is it possible?" "You are right."

The Gerards liked to talk. Madame Gerard, who was a good housekeeper, discussed questions of domestic economy; telling, for example, how she had been out that day, and had seen, upon the Rue du Bac, some merino: "A very good bargain, I assure you, Madame, and very wide!" Or perhaps the engraver, who was a simple politician, after the fashion of 1848, would declare that we must accept the Republic, "Oh, not the red-hot, you know, but the true, the real one!" Or he would wish that Cavaignac had been elected President at the September balloting; although he himself was then engraving—one must live, after all—a portrait of Prince Louis Napoleon, destined for the electoral platform. M. and Madame Violette let them talk; perhaps even they did not always pay attention to the conversation. When it was dark they held each other's hands and gazed at the stars.

These lovely, cool, autumnal evenings, upon the balcony, under the starry heavens, are the most distant of all Amedee's memories. Then there was a break in his memory, like a book with several leaves torn out, after which he recalls many sad days.

Winter had come, and they no longer spent their evenings upon the balcony. One could see nothing now through the windows but a dull, gray sky. Amedee's mother was ill and always remained in her bed. When he was installed near the bed, before a little table, cutting out with scissors the hussars from a sheet of Epinal, his poor mamma almost frightened him, as she leaned her elbow upon the pillow and gazed at him so long and so sadly, while her thin white hands restlessly pushed back her beautiful, disordered hair, and two red hectic spots burned under her cheekbones.

It was not she who now came to take him from his bed in the morning, but an old woman in a short jacket, who did not kiss him, and who smelled horribly of snuff.

His father, too, did not pay much attention to him now. When he returned in the evening from the office he always brought bottles and little packages from the apothecary. Sometimes he was accompanied by the physician, a large man, very much dressed and perfumed, who panted for breath after climbing the five flights of stairs. Once Amedee saw this stranger put his arms around his mother as she sat in her bed, and lay his head for a long time against her back. The child asked, "What for, mamma?"

M. Violette, more nervous than ever, and continually throwing back the rebellious lock behind his ear, would accompany the doctor to the door and stop there to talk with him. Then Amedee's mother would call to him, and he would climb upon the bed, where she would gaze at him with her bright eyes and press him to her breast, saying, in a sad tone, as if she pitied him: "My poor little Medee! My poor little Medee!" Why was it? What did it all mean?

His father would return with a forced smile which was pitiful to see.

"Well, what did the doctor say?"

"Oh, nothing, nothing! You are much better. Only, my poor Lucie, we must put on another blister to-night."

Oh, how monotonous and slow these days were to the little Amedee, near the drowsy invalid, in the close room smelling of drugs, where only the old snuff-taker entered once an hour to bring a cup of tea or put charcoal upon the fire!

Sometimes their neighbor, Madame Gerard, would come to inquire after the sick lady.

"Still very feeble, my good Madame Gerard," his mother would respond. "Ah, I am beginning to get discouraged."

But Madame Gerard would not let her be despondent.

"You see, Madame Violette, it is this horrible, endless winter. It is almost March now; they are already selling boxes of primroses in little carts on the sidewalks. You will surely be better as soon as the sun shines. If you like, I will take little Amedee back with me to play with my little girls. It will amuse the child."

So it happened that the good neighbor kept the child every afternoon, and he became very fond of the little Gerard children.

Four little rooms, that is all; but with a quantity of old, picturesque furniture; engravings, casts, and pictures painted by comrades were on the walls; the doors were always open, and the children could always play where they liked, chase each other through the apartments or pillage them. In the drawing-room, which had been transformed into a work-room, the artist sat upon a high stool, point in hand; the light from a curtainless window, sifting through the transparent paper, made the worthy man's skull shine as he leaned over his copper plate. He worked hard all day; with an expensive house and two girls to bring up, it was necessary. In spite of his advanced opinions, he continued to engrave his Prince Louis—"A rogue who is trying to juggle us out of a Republic." At the very most, he stopped only two or three times a day to smoke his Abu-el-Kader. Nothing distracted him from his work; not even the little ones, who, tired of playing their piece for four hands upon the piano, would organize, with Amedee, a game of hide-and-seek close by their father, behind the old Empire sofa ornamented with bronze lions' heads. But Madame Gerard, in her kitchen, where she was always cooking something good for dinner, sometimes thought they made too great an uproar. Then Maria, a real hoyden, in trying to catch her sister, would push an old armchair against a Renaissance chest and make all the Rouen crockery tremble.

"Now then, now then, children!" exclaimed Madame Gerard, from the depths of her lair, from which escaped a delicious odor of bacon. "Let your father have a little quiet, and go and play in the dining-room."

They obeyed; for there they could move chairs as they liked, build houses of them, and play at making calls. Did ever anybody have such wild ideas at five years of age as this Maria? She took the arm of Amedee, whom she called her little husband, and went to call upon her sister and show her her little child, a pasteboard doll with a large head, wrapped up in a napkin.

"As you see, Madame, it is a boy."

"What do you intend to make of him when he grows up?" asked Louise, who lent herself complacently to the play, for she was ten years old and quite a young lady, if you please.

"Why, Madame," replied Maria, gravely, "he will be a soldier."

At that moment the engraver, who had left his bench to stretch his legs a little and to light his Abd-el-Kader for the third time, came and stood at the threshold of his room. Madame Gerard, reassured as to the state of her stew, which was slowly cooking—and oh, how good it smelled in the kitchen!—entered the dining-room. Both looked at the children, so comical and so graceful, as they made their little grimaces! Then the husband glanced at his wife, and the wife at the husband, and both burst out into hearty laughter.

There never was any laughter in the apartment of the Violettes. It was cough! cough! cough! almost to suffocation, almost to death! This gentle young woman with the heavy hair was about to die! When the beautiful starry evenings should come again, she would no longer linger on the balcony, or press her husband's hand as they gazed at the stars. Little Amedee did not understand it; but he felt a vague terror of something dreadful happening in the house. Everything alarmed him now. He was afraid of the old woman who smelled of snuff, and who, when she dressed him in the morning, looked at him with a pitying air; he was afraid of the doctor, who climbed the five flights of stairs twice a day now, and left a whiff of perfume behind him; afraid of his father, who did not go to his office any more, whose beard was often three days old, and who feverishly paced the little parlor, tossing back with a distracted gesture the lock of hair behind his ear. He was afraid of his mother, alas! of his mother, whom he had seen that evening, by the light from the night-lamp, buried in the pillows, her delicate nose and chin thrown up, and who did not seem to recognize him, in spite of her wide-open eyes, when his father took her child in his arms and leaned over her with him that he might kiss her cold forehead covered with sweat!

At last the terrible day arrived, a day that Amedee never will forget, although he was then a very small child.

What awakened him that morning was his father's embrace as he came and took him from his bed. His father's eyes were wild and bloodshot from so much crying. Why was their neighbor, M. Gerard, there so early in the morning, and with great tears rolling down his cheeks too? He kept beside M. Violette, as if watching him, and patted him upon the back affectionately, saying:

"Now then, my poor friend! Have courage, courage!"

But the poor friend had no more. He let M. Gerard take the child from him, and then his head fell like a dead person's upon the good engraver's shoulder, and he began to weep with heavy sobs that shook his whole body.

"Mamma! See mamma!" cried the little Amedee, full of terror.

Alas! he never will see her again! At the Gerards, where they carried him and the kind neighbor dressed him, they told him that his mother had gone for a long time, a very long time; that he must love his papa very much and think only of him; and other things that he could not understand and dared not ask the meaning of, but which filled him with consternation.

It was strange! The engraver and his wife busied themselves entirely with him, watching him every moment. The little ones, too, treated him in a singular, almost respectful manner. What had caused such a change? Louise did not open her piano, and when little Maria wished to take her "menagerie" from the lower part of the buffet, Madame Gerard said sharply, as she wiped the tears from her eyes: "You must not play to-day."

After breakfast Madame Gerard put on her hat and shawl and went out, taking Amedee with her. They got into a carriage that took them through streets that the child did not know, across a bridge in the middle of which stood a large brass horseman, with his head crowned with laurel, and stopped before a large house and entered with the crowd, where a very agile and rapid young man put some black clothes on Amedee.

On their return the child found his father seated at the dining-room table with M. Gerard, and both of them were writing addresses upon large sheets of paper bordered with black. M. Violette was not crying, but his face showed deep lines of grief, and he let his lock of hair fall over his right eye.

At the sight of little Amedee, in his black clothes, he uttered a groan, and arose, staggering like a drunken man, bursting into tears again.

Oh, no! he never will forget that day, nor the horrible next day, when Madame Gerard came and dressed him in the morning in his black clothes, while he listened to the noise of heavy feet and blows from a hammer in the next room. He suddenly remembered that he had not seen his mother since two days before.

"Mamma! I want to see mamma!"

It was necessary then to try to make him understand the truth. Madame Gerard repeated to him that he ought to be very wise and good, and try to console his father, who had much to grieve him; for his mother had gone away forever; that she was in heaven.

In heaven! heaven is very high up and far off. If his mother was in heaven, what was it that those porters dressed in black carried away in the heavy box that they knocked at every turn of the staircase? What did that solemn carriage, which he followed through all the rain, quickening his childish steps, with his little hand tightly clasped in his father's, carry away? What did they bury in that hole, from which an odor of freshly dug earth was emitted—in that hole surrounded by men in black, and from which his father turned away his head in horror? What was it that they hid in this ditch, in this garden full of crosses and stone urns, where the newly budded trees shone in the March sun after the shower, large drops of water still falling from their branches like tears?

His mother was in heaven! On the evening of that dreadful day Amedee dared not ask to "see mamma" when he was seated before his father at the table, where, for a long time, the old woman in a short jacket had placed only two plates. The poor widower, who had just wiped his eyes with his napkin, had put upon one of the plates a little meat cut up in bits for Amedee. He was very pale, and as Amedee sat in his high chair, he asked himself whether he should recognize his mother's sweet, caressing look, some day, in one of those stars that she loved to watch, seated upon the balcony on cool September nights, pressing her husband's hand in the darkness.

CHAPTER II

SAD CHANGES

Trees are like men; there are some that have no luck. A genuinely unfortunate tree was the poor sycamore which grew in the playground of an institution for boys on the Rue de la Grande-Chaumiere, directed by M. Batifol.

Chance might just as well have made it grow upon the banks of a river, upon some pretty bluff, where it might have seen the boats pass; or, better still, upon the mall in some garrison village, where it could have had the pleasure of listening twice a week to military music. But, no! it was written in the book of fate that this unlucky sycamore should lose its bark every summer, as a serpent changes its skin, and should scatter the ground with its dead leaves at the first frost, in the playground of the Batifol institution, which was a place without any distractions.

This solitary tree, which was like any other sycamore, middle-aged and without any singularities, ought to have had the painful feeling that it served in a measure to deceive the public. In fact, upon the advertisement of the Batifol institution (Cours du lycee Henri IV. Preparation au baccalaureat et aux ecoles de l'Etat), one read these fallacious words, "There is a garden;" when in reality it was only a vulgar court graveled with stones from the river, with a paved gutter in which one could gather half a dozen of lost marbles, a broken top, and a certain number of shoe-nails, and after recreation hours still more. This solitary sycamore was supposed to justify the illusion and fiction of the garden promised in the advertisement; but as trees certainly have common sense, this one should have been conscious that it was not a garden of itself.

It was a very unjust fate for an inoffensive tree which never had harmed anybody; only expanding, at one side of the gymnasium portico, in a perfect rectangle formed by a prison wall, bristling with the glass of broken bottles, and by three buildings of distressing similarity, showing, above the numerous doors on the ground floor, inscriptions which merely to read induced a yawn: Hall 1, Hall 2, Hall 3, Hall 4, Stairway A, Stairway B, Entrance to the Dormitories, Dining-room, Laboratory.

The poor sycamore was dying of ennui in this dismal place. Its only happy seasons—the recreation hours, when the court echoed with the shouts and the laughter of the boys—were spoiled for it by the sight of two or three pupils who were punished by being made to stand at the foot of its trunk. Parisian birds, who are not fastidious, rarely lighted upon the tree, and never built their nests there. It might even be imagined that this disenchanted tree, when the wind agitated its foliage, would charitably say, "Believe me! the place is good for nothing. Go and make love elsewhere!"

In the shade of this sycamore, planted under an unlucky star, the greater part of Amedee's infancy was passed.

M. Violette was an employe of the Ministry, and was obliged to work seven hours a day, one or two hours of which were devoted to going wearily through a bundle of probably superfluous papers and documents. The rest of the time was given to other occupations as varied as they were intellectual; such as yawning, filing his nails, talking about his chiefs, groaning over the slowness of promotion, cooking a potato or a sausage in the stove for his luncheon, reading the newspaper down to the editor's signature, and advertisements in which some country cure expresses his artless gratitude at being cured at last of an obstinate disease. In recompense for this daily captivity, M. Violette received, at the end of the month, a sum exactly sufficient to secure his household soup and beef, with a few vegetables.

In order that his son might attain such a distinguished position, M. Violette's father, a watch-maker in Chartres, had sacrificed everything, and died penniless. The Silvio Pellico official, during these exasperating and tiresome hours, sometimes regretted not having simply succeeded his father. He could see himself, in imagination, in the light little shop near the cathedral, with a magnifying-glass fixed in his eye, ready to inspect some farmer's old "turnip," and suspended over his bench thirty silver and gold watches left by farmers the week before, who would profit by the next market-day to come and get them, all going together with a merry tick. It may be questioned whether a trade as low as this would have been fitting for a young man of education, a Bachelor of Arts, crammed with Greek roots and quotations, able to prove the existence of God, and to recite without hesitation the dates of the reigns of Nabonassar and of Nabopolassar. This watch-maker, this simple artisan, understood modern genius better. This modest shopkeeper acted according to the democratic law and followed the instinct of a noble and wise ambition. He made of his son—a sensible and intelligent boy—a machine to copy documents, and spend his days guessing the conundrums in the illustrated newspapers, which he read as easily as M. Ledrain would decipher the cuneiform inscriptions on an Assyrian brick. Also—an admirable result, which should rejoice the old watch-maker's shade—his son had become a gentleman, a functionary, so splendidly remunerated by the State that he was obliged to wear patches of cloth, as near like the trousers as possible, on their seat; and his poor young wife, during her life, had always been obliged, as rent-day drew near, to carry the soup-ladle and six silver covers to the pawn-shop.

At all events, M. Violette was a widower now, and being busy all day was very much embarrassed with the care of his little son. His neighbors, the Gerards, were very kind to Amedee, and continued to keep him with them all the afternoon. This state of affairs could not always continue, and M. Violette hesitated to abuse his worthy friends' kindness in that way.

However, Amedee gave them little trouble, and Mamma Gerard loved him as if he were her own. The orphan was now inseparable from little Maria, a perfect little witch, who became prettier every day. The engraver, having found in a cupboard the old bearskin cap which he had worn as a grenadier in the National Guard, a headdress that had been suppressed since '98, gave it to the children. What a magnificent plaything it was, and how well calculated to excite their imagination! It was immediately transformed in their minds into a frightfully large and ferocious bear, which they chased through the apartment, lying in wait for it behind armchairs, striking at it with sticks, and puffing out their little cheeks with all their might to say "Boum!" imitating the report of a gun. This hunting diversion completed the destruction of the old furniture. Tranquil in the midst of the joyous uproar and disorder, the engraver was busily at work finishing off the broad ribbon of the Legion of Honor, and the large bullion epaulettes of the Prince President, whom, as a suspicious republican and foreseeing the 'coup d'etat', he detested with all his heart.

"Truly, Monsieur Violette," said Mother Gerard to the employe, when he came for his little son upon his return from the office, and excused himself for the trouble that the child must give his neighbors, "truly, I assure you, he does not disturb us in the least. Wait a little before you send him to school. He is very quiet, and if Maria did not excite him so—upon my word, she is more of a boy than he—your Amedee would always be looking at the pictures. My Louise hears him read every day two pages in the Moral Tales, and yesterday he amused Gerard by telling him the story of the grateful elephant. He can go to school later—wait a little."

But M. Violette had decided to send Amedee to M. Batifol's. "Oh, yes, as a day scholar, of course! It is so convenient; not two steps' distance. This will not prevent little Amedee from seeing his friends often. He is nearly seven years old, and very backward; he hardly knows how to make his letters. One can not begin with children too soon," and much more to the same effect.

This was the reason why, one fine spring day, M. Violette was ushered into M. Batifol's office, who, the servant said, would be there directly.

M. Batifol's office was hideous. In the three bookcases which the master of the house—a snob and a greedy schoolmaster—never opened, were some of those books that one can buy upon the quays by the running yard; for example, Laharpe's Cours de Litterature, and an endless edition of Rollin, whose tediousness seems to ooze out through their bindings. The cylindrical office-table, one of those masterpieces of veneered mahogany which the Faubourg St. Antoine still keeps the secret of making, was surmounted by a globe of the world.

Suddenly, through the open window, little Amedee saw the sycamore in the yard. A young blackbird, who did not know the place, came and perched for an instant only upon one of its branches.

We may fancy the tree saying to it:

"What are you doing here? The Luxembourg is only a short distance from here, and is charming. Children are there, making mud-pies, nurses upon the seats chattering with the military, lovers promenading, holding hands. Go there, you simpleton!"

The blackbird flew away, and the university tree, once more solitary and alone, drooped its dispirited leaves. Amedee, in his confused childish desire for information, was just ready to ask why this sycamore looked so morose, when the door opened and M. Batifol appeared. The master of the school had a severe aspect, in spite of his almost indecorous name. He resembled a hippopotamus clothed in an ample black coat. He entered slowly and bowed in a dignified way to M. Violette, then seated himself in a leather armchair before his papers, and, taking off his velvet skull-cap, revealed such a voluminous round, yellow baldness that little Amedee compared it with terror to the globe on the top of his desk.

It was just the same thing! These two round balls were twins! There was even upon M. Batifol's cranium an eruption of little red pimples, grouped almost exactly like an archipelago in the Pacific Ocean.

"Whom have I the honor—?" asked the schoolmaster, in an unctuous voice, an excellent voice for proclaiming names at the distribution of prizes.

M. Violette was not a brave man. It was very foolish, but when the senior clerk called him into his office to do some work, he was always seized with a sort of stammering and shaking of the limbs. A person so imposing as M. Batifol was not calculated to give him assurance. Amedee was timid, too, like his father, and while the child, frightened by the resemblance of the sphere to M. Batifol's bald head, was already trembling, M. Violette, much agitated, was trying to think of something to say, consequently, he said nothing of any account. However, he ended by repeating almost the same things he had said to Mamma Gerard: "My son is nearly seven years old, and very backward, etc."

The teacher appeared to listen to M. Violette with benevolent interest, inclining his geographical cranium every few seconds. In reality, he was observing and judging his visitors. The father's scanty overcoat, the rather pale face of the little boy, all betokened poverty. It simply meant a day scholar at thirty francs a month, nothing more. So M. Batifol shortened the "speech" that under like circumstances he addressed to his new pupils.

He would take charge of his "young friend" (thirty francs a month, that is understood, and the child will bring his own luncheon in a little basket) who would first be placed in an elementary class. Certain fathers prefer, and they have reason to do so, that their sons should be half-boarders, with a healthful and abundant repast at noon. But M. Batifol did not insist upon it. His young friend would then be placed in the infant class, at first; but he would be prepared there at once, 'ab ovo', one day to receive lessons in this University of France, 'alma parens' (instruction in foreign languages not included in the ordinary price, naturally), which by daily study, competition between scholars (accomplishments, such as dancing, music, and fencing, to be paid for separately; that goes without saying) prepare children for social life, and make men and citizens of them.

M. Violette contented himself with the day school at thirty francs, and for a good reason. The affair was settled. Early the next morning Amedee would enter the "ninth preparatory."

"Give me your hand, my young friend," said the master, as father and son arose to take their leave.

Amedee reached out his hand, and M. Batifol took it in his, which was so heavy, large, and cold that the child shivered at the contact, and fancied he was touching a leg of mutton of six or seven pounds' weight, freshly killed, and sent from the butcher's.

Finally they left. Early the next morning, Amedee, provided with a little basket, in which the old snuff-taker had put a little bottle of red wine, and some sliced veal, and jam tarts, presented himself at the boarding-school, to be prepared without delay for the teaching of the 'alma parens'.

The hippopotamus clothed in black did not take off his skullcap this time, to the child's great regret, for he wished to assure himself if the degrees of latitude and longitude were checked off in squares on M. Batifol's cranium as they were on the terrestrial globe. He conducted his pupil to his class at once and presented him to the master.

"Here is a new day scholar, Monsieur Tavernier. You will find out how far advanced he is in reading and writing, if you please." M. Tavernier was a tall young man with a sallow complexion, a bachelor who, had he been living like his late father, a sergeant of the gendarmes, in a pretty house surrounded by apple trees and green grass, would not, perhaps, have had that 'papier-mache' appearance, and would not have been dressed at eight o'clock in the morning in a black coat of the kind we see hanging in the Morgue. M. Tavernier received the newcomer with a sickly smile, which disappeared as soon as M. Batifol left the room.

"Go and take your place in that empty seat there, in the third row," said M. Tavernier, in an indifferent tone.

He deigned, however, to conduct Amedee to the seat which he was to occupy. Amedee's neighbor, one of the future citizens preparing for social life—several with patches upon their trousers—had been naughty enough to bring into class a handful of cockchafers. He was punished by a quarter of an hour's standing up, which he did soon after, sulking at the foot of the sycamore-tree in the large court.

"You will soon see what a cur he is," whispered the pupil in disgrace; as soon as the teacher had returned to his seat.

M. Tavernier struck his ruler on the edge of his chair, and, having reestablished silence, invited pupil Godard to recite his lesson.

Pupil Godard, who was a chubby-faced fellow with sleepy eyes, rose automatically and in one single stream, like a running tap, recited, without stopping to take breath, "The Wolf and the Lamb," rolling off La Fontaine's fable like the thread from a bobbin run by steam.

"The-strongest-reason-is-always-the-best-and-we-will-prove-it-at-once-a-lamb-was-quenching-his-thirst-in-a-stream-of-pure-running-water—"

Suddenly Godard was confused, he hesitated. The machine had been badly oiled. Something obstructed the bobbin.

"In-a-stream-of-pure-running-water-in-a stream—"

Then he stopped short, the tap was closed. Godard did not know his lesson, and he, too, was condemned to remain on guard under the sycamore during recess.

After pupil Godard came pupil Grosdidier; then Blanc, then Moreau (Gaston), then Moreau (Ernest), then Malepert; then another, and another, who babbled with the same intelligence and volubility, with the same piping voice, this cruel and wonderful fable. It was as irritating and monotonous as a fine rain. All the pupils in the "ninth preparatory" were disgusted for fifteen years, at least, with this most exquisite of French poems.

Little Amedee wanted to cry; he listened with stupefaction blended with fright as the scholars by turns unwound their bobbins. To think that to-morrow he must do the same! He never would be able. M. Tavernier frightened him very much, too. The yellow-complexioned usher, seated nonchalantly in his armchair, was not without pretension; in spite of his black coat with the "take-me-out-of-pawn" air, polished his nails, and only opened his mouth at times to utter a reprimand or pronounce sentence of punishment.

This was school, then! Amedee recalled the pleasant reading-lessons that the eldest of the Gerards had given him—that good Louise, so wise and serious and only ten years old, pointing out his letters to him in a picture alphabet with a knitting-needle, always so patient and kind. The child was overcome at the very first with a disgust for school, and gazed through the window which lighted the room at the noiselessly moving, large, indented leaves of the melancholy sycamore.

CHAPTER III

PAPA AND MAMMA GERARD

One, two, three years rolled by without anything very remarkable happening to the inhabitants of the fifth story.

The quarter had not changed, and it still had the appearance of a suburban faubourg. They had just erected, within gunshot of the house where the Violettes and Gerards lived, a large five-story building, upon whose roof still trembled in the wind the masons' withered bouquets. But that was all. In front of them, on the lot "For Sale," enclosed by rotten boards, where one could always see tufts of nettles and a goat tied to a stake, and upon the high wall above which by the end of April the lilacs hung in their perfumed clusters, the rains had not effaced this brutal declaration of love, scraped with a knife in the plaster: "When Melie wishes she can have me," and signed "Eugene."

Three years had passed, and little Amedee had grown a trifle. At that time a child born in the centre of Paris—for example, in the labyrinth of infected streets about the Halles—would have grown up without having any idea of the change of seasons other than by the state of the temperature and the narrow strip of sky which he could see by raising his head. Even today certain poor children—the poor never budge from their hiding-places—learn of the arrival of winter only by the odor of roasted chestnuts; of spring, by the boxes of gilly-flowers in the fruiterer's stall; of summer, by the water-carts passing, and of autumn, by the heaps of oyster-shells at the doors of wine-shops. The broad sky, with its confused shapes of cloud architecture, the burning gold of the setting sun behind the masses of trees, the enchanting stillness of moonlight upon the river, all these grand and magnificent spectacles are for the delight of those who live in suburban quarters, or play there sometimes. The sons of people who work in buttons and jet spend their infancy playing on staircases that smell of lead, or in courts that resemble wells, and do not suspect that nature exists. At the outside they suspect that nature may exist when they see the horses on Palm Sunday decorated with bits of boxwood behind each ear. What matters it, after all, if the child has imagination? A star reflected in a gutter will reveal to him an immense nocturnal poem; and he will breathe all the intoxication of summer in the full-blown rose which the grisette from the next house lets fall from her hair.

Amedee had had the good fortune of being born in that delicious and melancholy suburb of Paris which had not yet become "Haussmannized," and was full of wild and charming nooks.

His father, the widower, could not be consoled, and tried to wear out his grief in long promenades, going out on clear evenings, holding his little boy by the hand, toward the more solitary places. They followed those fine boulevards, formerly in the suburbs, where there were giant elms, planted in the time of Louis XIV, ditches full of grass, ruined palisades, showing through their opening market-gardens where melons glistened in the rays of the setting sun. Both were silent; the father lost in reveries, Amedee absorbed in the confused dreams of a child. They went long distances, passing the Barriere d'Enfer, reaching unknown parts, which produced the same effect upon an inhabitant of Rue Montmartre as the places upon an old map of the world, marked with the mysterious words 'Mare ignotum', would upon a savant of the Middle Ages. There were many houses in this ancient suburb; curious old buildings, nearly all of one story.

Sometimes they would pass a public-house painted in a sinister wine-color; or else a garden hedged in by acacias, at the fork of two roads, with arbors and a sign consisting of a very small windmill at the end of a pole, turning in the fresh evening breeze. It was almost country; the grass grew upon the sidewalks, springing up in the road between the broken pavements. A poppy flashed here and there upon the tops of the low walls. They met very few people; now and then some poor person, a woman in a cap dragging along a crying child, a workman burdened with his tools, a belated invalid, and sometimes in the middle. of the sidewalk, in a cloud of dust, a flock of exhausted sheep, bleating desperately, and nipped in the legs by dogs hurrying them toward the abattoir. The father and son would walk straight ahead until it was dark under the trees; then they would retrace their steps, the sharp air stinging their faces. Those ancient hanging street-lamps, the tragic lanterns of the time of the Terror, were suspended at long intervals in the avenue, mingling their dismal twinkle with the pale gleams of the green twilight sky.

These sorrowful promenades with his melancholy companion would commonly end a tiresome day at Batifol's school. Amedee was now in the "seventh," and knew already that the phrase, "the will of God," could not be turned into Latin by 'bonitas divina', and that the word 'cornu' was not declinable. These long, silent hours spent at his school-desk, or beside a person absorbed in grief, might have become fatal to the child's disposition, had it not been for his good friends, the Gerards. He went to see them as often as he was able, a spare hour now and then, and most of the day on Thursdays. The engraver's house was always full of good-nature and gayety, and Amedee felt comfortable and really happy there.

The good Gerards, besides their Louise and Maria, to say nothing of Amedee, whom they looked upon as one of the family, had now taken charge of a fourth child, a little girl, named Rosine, who was precisely the same age as their youngest.

This was the way it happened. Above the Gerards, in one of the mansards upon the sixth floor, lived a printer named Combarieu, with his wife or mistress—the concierge did not know which, nor did it matter much. The woman had just deserted him, leaving a child of eight years. One could expect nothing better of a creature who, according to the concierge, fed her husband upon pork-butcher's meat, to spare herself the trouble of getting dinner, and passed the entire day with uncombed hair, in a dressing-sacque, reading novels, and telling her fortune with cards. The grocer's daughter declared she had met her one evening, at a dancing-hall, seated with a fireman before a salad-bowl full of wine, prepared in the French fashion.

During the day Combarieu, although a red-hot Republican, sent his little girl to the Sisters; but he went out every evening with a mysterious air and left the child alone. The concierge even uttered in a low voice, with the romantic admiration which that class of people have for conspirators, the terrible word "secret society," and asserted that the printer had a musket concealed under his straw bed.

These revelations were of a nature to excite M. Gerard's sympathy in favor of his neighbor, for the coup d'etat and the proclamation of the Empire had irritated him very much. Had it not been his melancholy duty to engrave, the day after the second of December—he must feed his family first of all—a Bonapartist allegory entitled, "The Uncle and the Nephew," where one saw France extending its hand to Napoleon I and Prince Louis, while soaring above the group was an eagle with spreading wings, holding in one of his claws the cross of the Legion of Honor?

One day the engraver asked his wife, as he lighted his pipe—he had given up Abd-el-Kader and smoked now a Barbes—if they ought not to interest themselves a little in the abandoned child. It needed nothing more to arouse the good woman, who had already said more than once: "What a pity!" as she saw little Rosine waiting for her father in the lodge of the concierge, asleep in a chair before the stove. She coaxed the child to play with her children. Rosine was very pretty, with bright eyes, a droll little Parisian nose, and a mass of straw-colored curly hair escaping from her cap. The little rogue let fly quite often some gutter expression, such as "Hang it!" or "Tol-derol-dol!" at which Madame Gerard would exclaim, "What do I hear, Mademoiselle?" but she was intelligent and soon corrected herself.

One Sunday morning, Combarieu, having learned of their kindness to his child, made a visit to thank them.

Very dark, with a livid complexion, all hair and beard, and trying to look like the head of Jesus Christ, in his long black blouse he embodied the type of a club conspirator, a representative of the workingmen. A Freemason, probably; a solemn drunkard, who became intoxicated oftener on big words than on native wine, and spoke in a loud, pretentious voice, gazing before him with large, stupid eyes swimming in a sort of ecstasy; his whole person made one think of a boozy preacher. He immediately inspired the engraver with respect, and dazzled him by the fascination which the audacious exert over the timid. M. Gerard thought he discerned in Combarieu one of those superior men whom a cruel fate had caused to be born among the lower class and in whom poverty had stifled genius.

Enlightened as to the artist's political preferences by the bowl of his pipe, Combarieu complacently eulogized himself. Upon his own admission he had at first been foolish enough to dream of a universal brotherhood, a holy alliance of the people. He had even written poems which he had published himself, notably an "Ode to Poland," and an "Epistle to Beranger," which latter had evoked an autograph letter from the illustrious song-writer. But he was no longer such a simpleton.

"When one has seen what we have seen during June, and on the second of December, there is no longer any question of sentiment." Here the engraver, as a hospitable host, brought a bottle of wine and two glasses. "No, Monsieur Gerard, I thank you, I take nothing between my meals. The workingmen have been deceived too often, and at the next election we shall not let the bourgeoisie strangle the Republic." (M. Gerard had now uncorked the bottle.) "Only a finger! Enough! Enough! simply so as not to refuse you. While waiting, let us prepare ourselves. Just now the Eastern question muddles us, and behold 'Badinguet,'—[A nickname given to Napoleon III.]—with a big affair upon his hands. You have some wine here that is worth drinking. If he loses one battle he is done for. One glass more? Ah! you make me depart from my usual custom—absolutely done for. But this time we shall keep our eyes open. No half measures! We will return to the great methods of 'ninety-three—the Committee of Public Safety, the Law of Suspects, the Revolutionary Tribunal, every damned one of them! and, if it is necessary, a permanent guillotine! To your good health!"

So much energy frightened Father Gerard a little; for in spite of his Barbes pipe-bowl he was not a genuine red-hot Republican. He dared not protest, however, and blushed a little as he thought that the night before an editor had proposed to him to engrave a portrait of the new Empress, very decollete, and showing her famous shoulders, and that he had not said No; for his daughters needed new shoes, and his wife had declared the day before that she had not a gown to put on.

So for several months he had four children—Amedee, Louise, Maria, and little Rose Combarieu—to make a racket in his apartment. Certainly they were no longer babies; they did not play at making calls nor chase the old fur hat around the room; they were more sensible, and the old furniture had a little rest. And it was time, for all the chairs were lame, two of the larger ones had lost an arm each, and the Empire sofa had lost the greater part of its hair through the rents in its dark-green velvet covering. The unfortunate square piano had had no pity shown it; more out of tune and asthmatic than ever, it was now always open, and one could read above the yellow and worn-out keyboard a once famous name-"Sebastian Erard, Manufacturer of Pianos and Harps for S.A.R. Madame la Duchesse de Berri." Not only Louise, the eldest of the Gerards—a large girl now, having been to her first communion, dressing her hair in bands, and wearing white waists—not only Louise, who had become a good musician, had made the piano submit to long tortures, but her sister Maria, and Amedee also, already played the 'Bouquet de Bal' or 'Papa, les p'tits bateaux'. Rosine, too, in her character of street urchin, knew all the popular songs, and spent entire hours in picking out the airs with one finger upon the old instrument.

Ah! the songs of those days, the last of romanticism, the make-believe 'Orientales'; 'Odes' and 'Ballads', by the dozen; 'Comes d'Espagne et d'Italie', with their pages, turrets, chatelaines; bull-fighters, Spanish ladies; vivandieres, beguiled away from their homes under the pale of the church, "near a stream of running water, by a gay and handsome chevalier," and many other such silly things—Amedee will remember them always! They bring back to him, clearly and strongly, certain happy hours in his childhood! They make him smell again at times even the odor that pervaded the Gerards' house. A mule-driver's song will bring up before his vision the engraver working at his plate before the curtainless window on a winter's day. It snows in the streets, and large white flakes are slowly falling behind the glass; but the room, ornamented with pictures and busts, is lighted and heated by a bright coke fire. Amedee can see himself seated in a corner by the fire, learning by heart a page of the "Epitome" which he must recite the next morning at M. Batifol's. Maria and Rosine are crouched at his feet, with a box of glass beads, which they are stringing into a necklace. It was comfortable; the whole apartment smelled of the engraver's pipe, and in the dining-room, whose door is half opened, Louise is at the piano, singing, in a fresh voice, some lines where "Castilla" rhymes with "mantilla," and "Andalousie" with "jealousy," while her agile fingers played on the old instrument an accompaniment supposed to imitate bells and castanets.

Or perhaps it is a radiant morning in June, and they are in the dining-room; the balcony door is open wide, and a large hornet buzzes loudly in the vine. Louise is still at the piano; she is singing this time, and trying to reach the low tones of a dramatic romance where a Corsican child is urged on to vengeance by his father:

Tiens, prends ma carabiue!
Sur toi veillera Dieu—

This is a great day, the day when Mamma Gerard makes her gooseberry preserves. There is a large basin already full of it on the table. What a delicious odor! A perfume of roses mingled with that of warm sugar. Maria and Rosine have just slipped into the kitchen, the gourmands! But Louise is a serious person, and will not interrupt her singing for such a trifle. She continues to sing in a low voice: and at the moment when Amedee stands speechless with admiration before her, as she is scolding in a terrible tone and playing dreadful chords, to and behold! here come the children, both with pink moustaches, and licking their lips voluptuously.

Ah! these were happy hours to Amedee. They consoled him for the interminable days at M. Batifol's.

Having passed the ninth preparatory grade, under the direction of the indolent M. Tavernier, always busy polishing his nails, like a Chinese mandarin, the child had for a professor in the eighth grade Pere Montandeuil, a poor fellow stupefied by thirty years of teaching, who secretly employed all his spare hours in composing five-act tragedies, and who, by dint of carrying to and going for his manuscripts at the Odeon, ended by marrying the stagedoor-keeper's daughter. In the seventh grade Amedee groaned under the tyranny of M. Prudhommod, a man from the country, with a smattering of Latin and a terribly violent temper, throwing at the pupils the insults of a plowboy. Now he had entered the sixth grade, under M. Bance, an unfortunate fellow about twenty years old, ugly, lame, and foolishly timid, whom M. Batifol reproached severely with not having made himself respected, and whose eyes filled with tears every morning when, upon entering the schoolroom, he was obliged to efface with a cloth a caricature of himself made by some of his pupils.

Everything in M. Batifol's school—the grotesque and miserable teachers, the ferocious and cynical pupils, the dingy, dusty, and ink-stained rooms—saddened and displeased Amedee. Although very intelligent, he was disgusted with the sort of instruction there, which was served out in portions, like soldier's rations, and would have lost courage but for his little friend, Louise Gerard, who out of sheer kindness constituted herself his school-mistress, guiding and inspiriting him, and working hard at the rudiments of L'homond's Grammar and Alexandre's Dictionary, to help the child struggle with his 'De Viris'. Unfortunate indeed is he who has not had, during his infancy, a petticoat near him—the sweet influence of a woman. He will always have something coarse in his mind and hard in his heart. Without this excellent and kind Louise, Amedee would have been exposed to this danger. His mother was dead, and M. Violette, alas! was always overwhelmed with his grief, and, it must be admitted, somewhat neglected his little son.

The widower could not be consoled. Since his wife's death he had grown ten years older, and his refractory lock of hair had become perfectly white. His Lucie had been the sole joy in his commonplace and obscure life. She was so pretty, so sweet! such a good manager, dressing upon nothing, and making things seem luxurious with only one flower! M. Violette existed only on this dear and cruel souvenir, living his humble idyll over again in his mind.

He had had six years of this happiness. One of his comrades took him to pass an evening with an old friend who was captain in the Invalides. The worthy man had lost an arm at Waterloo; he was a relative of Lucie, a good-natured old fellow, amiable and lively, delighting in arranging his apartments into a sort of Bonapartist chapel and giving little entertainments with cake and punch, while Lucie's mother, a cousin of the captain, did the honors. M. Violette immediately observed the young girl, seated under a "Bataille des Pyramides" with two swords crossed above it, a carnation in her hair. It was in midsummer, and through the open window one could see the magnificent moonlight, which shone upon the esplanade and made the huge cannon shine. They were playing charades, and when it came Lucie's turn to be questioned among all the guests, M. Violette, to relieve her of her embarrassment, replied so awkwardly that they all exclaimed, "Now, then, that is cheating!" With what naive grace and bashful coquetry she served the tea, going from one table to another, cup in hand, followed by the one-armed captain with silver epaulets, carrying the plum-cake! In order to see her again, M. Violette paid the captain visit after visit. But the greater part of the time he saw only the old soldier, who told him of his victories and conquests, of the attack of the redoubt at Borodino, and the frightful swearing of the dashing Murat, King of Naples, as he urged the squadrons on to the rescue. At last, one beautiful Sunday in autumn, he found himself alone with the young girl in the private garden of the veteran of the Old Guard. He seated himself beside Lucie on a stone bench: he told her his love, with the profound gaze of the Little Corporal, in bronzed plaster, resting upon them; and, full of delicious confusion, she replied, "Speak to mamma," dropping her bewildered eyes and gazing at the bed of china-asters, whose boxwood border traced the form of a cross of the Legion of Honor.

And all this was effaced, lost forever! The captain was dead; Lucie's mother was dead, and Lucie herself, his beloved Lucie, was dead, after giving him six years of cloudless happiness.

Certainly, he would never marry again. Oh, never!

No woman had ever existed or ever would exist for him but his poor darling, sleeping in the Montparnasse Cemetery, whose grave he visited every Sunday with a little watering-pot concealed under his coat.

He recalled, with a shiver of disgust, how, a few months after Lucie's death, one stifling evening in July, he was seated upon a bench in the Luxembourg, listening to the drums beating a retreat under the trees, when a woman came and took a seat beside him and looked at him steadily. Surprised by her significant look, he replied, to the question that she addressed to him, timidly and at the same time boldly: "So this is the way that you take the air?" And when she ended by asking him, "Come to my house," he had followed her. But he had hardly entered when the past all came back to him, and he felt a stifled feeling of distress. Falling into a chair, he sobbed, burying his face in his hands. His grief was so violent that, by a feminine instinct of pity, the wretched creature took his head in her arms, saying, in a consoling tone, "There, cry, cry, it will do you good!" and rocked him like an infant. At last he disengaged himself from this caress, which made him ashamed of himself, and throwing what little money he had about him upon the top of the bureau, he went away and returned to his home, where he went hastily to bed and wept to his heart's content, as he gnawed his pillow. Oh, horrible memories!

No! never a wife, no mistress, nothing! Now his grief was his wife, and lived with him.

The widower's morning awakening was frightful above all things else-his awakening in the large bed that now had but one pillow. It was there that he had once had the exquisite pleasure of watching his dear Lucie every morning when asleep; for she did not like to get up early, and sometimes he had jokingly scolded her for it. What serenity upon this delicate, sweet face, with its closed eyes, nestling among her beautiful, disordered hair! How chaste this lovely young wife was in her unconstraint! She had thrown one of her arms outside of the covering, and the neck of her nightrobe, having slipped down, showed such a pure white shoulder and delicate neck. He leaned over the half-opened mouth, which exhaled a warm and living odor, something like the perfume of a flower, to inhale it, and a tender pride swept over him when he thought that she was his, his wife, this delicious creature who was almost a child yet, and that her heart was given to him forever. He could not resist it; he touched his young wife's lips with his own. She trembled under the kiss and opened her eyes, when the astonishment of the awakening was at once transformed into a happy smile as she met her husband's glance. Oh, blissful moment! But in spite of all, one must be sensible. He recalled that the milk-maid had left at daybreak her pot of milk at the door of their apartment; that the fire was not lighted, and that he must be at the office early, as the time for promotions was drawing near. Giving another kiss to the half-asleep Lucie, he said to her, in a coaxing tone, "Now then, Lucie, my child, it is half-past eight. Up, up with you, lazy little one!"

How could he console himself for such lost happiness? He had his son, yes—and he loved him very much—but the sight of Amedee increased M. Violette's grief; for the child grew to look more like his mother every day.

CHAPTER IV

THE DEMON ABSINTHE

Three or four times a year M. Violette, accompanied by his son, paid a visit to an uncle of his deceased wife, whose heir Amedee might some day become.

M. Isidore Gaufre had founded and made successful a large house for Catholic books and pictures, to which he had added an important agency for the sale of all kinds of religious objects. This vast establishment was called, by a stroke of genius of its proprietor, "Bon Marche des Paroisses," and was famous among all the French clergy. At last it occupied the principal part of the house and all the out-buildings of an old hotel on the Rue Servandoni, constructed in the pompous and magnificent style of the latter part of the seventeenth century. He did a great business there.

All day long, priests and clerical-looking gentlemen mounted the long flight of steps that led to a spacious first floor, lighted by large, high windows surmounted by grotesque heads. There the long-bearded missionaries came to purchase their cargoes of glass beads or imitation coral rosaries, before embarking for the East, or the Gaboon, to convert the negroes and the Chinese.

The member of the third estate, draped in a long chocolate-colored, straight frock-coat, holding a gigantic umbrella under his arm, procured, dirt cheap and by the thousand, pamphlets of religious tenets. The country curate, visiting Paris, arranged for the immediate delivery of a remonstrance, in electrotype, Byzantine style, signing a series of long-dated bills, contracting, by zeal supplemented by some ready cash, to fulfil his liabilities, through the generosity of the faithful ones.

There, likewise, a young director of consciences came to look for some devotional work—for example, the 12mo entitled "Widows' Tears Wiped Away," by St. Francois de Sales—for some penitent. The representative from some deputation from a devoutly Catholic district would solicit a reduction upon a purchase of the "Twelve Stations of the Cross," hideously daubed, which he proposed to present to the parishes which his adversaries had accused of being Voltairians. A brother of the Christian Doctrine, or a sister of St. Vincent de Paul, would bargain for catechisms for their schools. From time to time, even a prince of the church, a bishop with aristocratic mien, enveloped in an ample gown, with his hat surrounded with a green cord and golden tassels, would mysteriously shut himself up in M. Isidore Gaufre's office for an hour; and then would be reconducted to the top of the steps by the cringing proprietor, profuse with his "Monseigneur," and obsequiously bowing under the haughty benediction of two fingers in a violet glove.

It was certainly not from sympathy that M. Violette had kept up his relations with his wife's uncle; for M. Gaufre, who was servilely polite to all those in whom he had an interest, was usually disdainful, sometimes even insolent, to those who were of no use to him. During his niece's life he had troubled himself very little about her, and had given her for a wedding present only an ivory crucifix with a shell for holy water, such as he sold by the gross to be used in convents. A self-made man, having already amassed—so they said—a considerable fortune, M. Gaufre held in very low estimation this poor devil of a commonplace employe whose slow advancement was doubtless due to the fact that he was lazy and incapable. From the greeting that he received, M. Violette suspected the poor opinion that M. Gaufre had of him. If he went there in spite of his natural pride it was only on his son's account. For M. Gaufre was rich, and he was not young. Perhaps—who could tell?—he might not forget Amedee, his nephew, in his will? It was necessary for him to see the child occasionally, and M. Violette, in pursuance of his paternal duty, condemned himself, three or four times a year, to the infliction of a visit at the "Bon Marche des Paroisses."

The hopes that M. Violette had formed as to his son's inheriting from M. Gaufre were very problematical; for the father, whom M. Gaufre had not been able to avoid receiving at his table occasionally, had been struck, even shocked, by the familiar and despotic tone of the old merchant's servant, a superb Normandy woman of about twenty-five years, answering to the royal name of Berenice. The impertinent ways of this robust woman betrayed her position in her master's house, as much as the diamonds that glittered in her ears. This creature would surely watch the will of her patron, a sexagenarian with an apoplectic neck, which became the color of dregs of wine after a glass of brandy.

M. Gaufre, although very practical and a churchwarden at St. Sulpice, had always had a taste for liaisons. His wife, during her life—he had been a widower for a dozen years—had been one of those unfortunate beings of whom people said, "That poor lady is to be pitied; she never can keep a servant." She had in vain taken girls from the provinces, without beauty and certified to be virtuous. One by one—a Flemish girl, an Alsatian, three Nivernaise, two from Picardy; even a young girl from Beauce, hired on account of her certificate as "the best-behaved girl in the village"—they were unsparingly devoured by the minotaur of the Rue Servandoni. All were turned out of doors, with a conscientious blow in the face, by the justly irritated spouse. When he became a widower he gave himself up to his liaisons in perfect security, but without scandal, of course, as to his passion for servants. New country-girls, wearing strange headdresses, responded favorably, in various patois, to his propositions. An Alsatian bow reigned six months; a Breton cap more than a year; but at last what must inevitably take place happened. The beautiful Berenice definitely bound with fetters of iron the old libertine. She was now all-powerful in the house, where she reigned supreme through her beauty and her talent for cooking; and as she saw her master's face grow more congested at each repast, she made her preparations for the future. Who could say but that M. Gaufre, a real devotee after all, would develop conscientious scruples some day, and end in a marriage, in extremis?

M. Violette knew all this; nevertheless it was important that Amedee should not be forgotten by his old relative, and sometimes, though rarely, he would leave his office a little earlier than usual, call for his son as he left the Batifol boarding-school, and take him to the Rue Servandoni.

The large drawing-rooms, transformed into a shop, where one could still see, upon forgotten panels, rococo shepherds offering doves to their shepherdesses, were always a new subject of surprise to little Amedee. After passing through the book-shop, where thousands of little volumes with figured gray and yellow covers crowded the shelves, and boys in ecru linen blouses were rapidly tying up bundles, one entered the jewellery department. There, under beautiful glass cases, sparkled all the glittering display and showy luxury of the Church, golden tabernacles where the Paschal Lamb reposed in a flaming triangle, censers with quadruple chains, stoles and chasubles, heavy with embroidery, enormous candelabra, ostensories and drinking-cups incrusted with enamel and false precious stones-before all these splendors the child, who had read the Arabian Nights, believed that he had entered Aladdin's cave, or Aboul-Cassem's pit. From this glittering array one passed, without transition, into the sombre depot of ecclesiastical vestments. Here all was black. One saw only piles of cassocks and pyramids of black hats. Two manikins, one clothed in a cardinal's purple robe, the other in episcopalian violet, threw a little color over the gloomy show.

But the large hall with painted statues amazed Amedee. They were all there, statues of all the saints in little chapels placed promiscuously upon the shelves in rows.

No more hierarchy. The Evangelist had, for a neighbor a little Jesuit saint—an upstart of yesterday. The unfortunate Fourier had at his side the Virgin Mary. The Saviour of men elbowed St. Labre. They were of plaster run into moulds, or roughly carved in wood, and were colored with paint as glaring as the red and blue of a barber's pole, and covered with vulgar gildings. Chins in the air, ecstatic eyes shining with varnish, horribly ugly and all new, they were drawn up in line like recruits at the roll-call, the mitred bishop, the martyr carrying his palm, St. Agnes embracing her lamb, St. Roch with his dog and shells, St. John the Baptist in his sheepskin, and, most ridiculous of all, poor Vincent de Paul carrying three naked children in his arms, like a midwife's advertisement.

This frightful exhibition, which was of the nature of the Tussaud Museum or a masquerade, positively frightened Amedee. He had recently been to his first communion, and was still burning with the mystical fever, but so much ugliness offended his already fastidious taste and threw him into his first doubt.

One day, about five o'clock, M. Violette and his son arrived at the "Bon Marche des Paroisses," and found Uncle Isidore in the room where the painted statues were kept, superintending—the packing of a St. Michel. The last customer of the day was just leaving, the Bishop 'in partibus' of Trebizonde, blessing M. Gaufre. The little apoplectic man, the giver of holy water, left alone with his clerks, felt under restraint no longer.

"Pay attention, you confounded idiot!" he cried to the young man just ready to lay the archangel in the shavings. "You almost broke the dragon's tail."

Then, noticing Amedee and M. Violette who had just entered:

"Ah! It is you, Violate! Good-day! Good-day, Amedee! You come at an unlucky time. It is shipping-day with us. I am in a great hurry—Eh! Monsieur Combier, by your leave, Monsieur Combier! Do not forget the three dozen of the Apparition de la Salette in stucco for Grenoble, with twenty-five per cent. reduction upon the bill. Are you working hard, Amedee? What do you say? He was first and assisted at the feast of St. Charlemagne! So much the better!—Jules, did you send the six chandeliers and the plated pyx and the Stations of the Cross, Number Two, to the Dames du Sacre-Coeur d'Alencons? What, not yet? But the order came three days ago! You must hurry, I tell you!—You can see, Violette, I am overflowing with work—but come in here a moment."

And once more ordering his bookkeeper, a captive in his glass case, to send the officers the notes that the cure of Sourdeval had allowed to go to protest, Uncle Isidore ushered M. Violette and his son into his office.

It was an ancient room, and M. Gaufre, who aimed at the austere, had made it gloomier still by a safe, and black haircloth furniture, which looked as if taken from a vestryroom. The pretty, high, and oval apartment, with its large window, opening upon a garden, its ceiling painted in light rosy clouds, its woodwork ornamented with wreaths and quivers, still preserved some of the charm and elegance of former days. Amedee would have been amused there, had not Uncle Isidore, who had seated himself before his desk, launched at once an unkind question at M. Violette.

"By the way, have you obtained the promotion that you counted so much upon last year?"

"Unfortunately, no, Monsieur Gaufre. You know what the Administration is."

"Yes, it is slow; but you are not overwhelmed with work, however. While in a business like this—what cares, what annoyances! I sometimes envy you. You can take an hour to cut your pens. Well, what is wanted of me now?"

The head of a clerk with a pencil behind his ear, appeared through the half-open door.

"Monsieur le Superieur of Foreign Missions wishes to speak with Monsieur."

"You can see! Not one minute to myself. Another time, my dear Violette. Adieu, my little man—it is astonishing how much he grows to look like Lucie! You must come and dine with me some Sunday, without ceremony. Berenice's 'souffle au fromage' is something delicious! Let Monsieur le Superieur come in."

M. Violette took his departure, displeased at his useless visit and irritated against Uncle Isidore, who had been hardly civil.

"That man is a perfect egotist," thought he, sadly; "and that girl has him in her clutches. My poor Amedee will have nothing from him."

Amedee himself was not interested in his uncle's fortune. He was just then a pupil in the fourth grade, which follows the same studies as at the Lycee Henri IV. Having suddenly grown tall, he was annoyed at wearing short trousers, and had already renounced all infantile games. The dangling crows which illustrated the pages of his Burnouf grammar were all dated the previous year, and he had entirely renounced feeding silkworms in his desk. Everything pointed to his not being a very practical man. Geometry disgusted him, and as for dates, he could not remember one. On holidays he liked to walk by himself through quiet streets; he read poems at the bookstalls, and lingered in the Luxembourg

Gardens to see the sun set. Destined to be a dreamer and a sentimentalist—so much the worse for you, poor Amedee!

He went very often to the Gerards, but he no longer called his little friends "thou." Louise was now seventeen years old, thin, without color, and with a lank figure; decidedly far from pretty. People, in speaking of her, began to say, "She has beautiful eyes and is an excellent musician." Her sister Maria was twelve years old and a perfect little rosebud.

As to the neighbor's little girl, Rosine Combarieu, she had disappeared. One day the printer suddenly departed without saying a word to anybody, and took his child with him. The concierge said that he was concerned in some political plot, and was obliged to leave the house in the night. They believed him to be concealed in some small town.

Accordingly, Father Gerard was not angry with him for fleeing without taking leave of him. The conspirator had kept all his prestige in the eyes of the engraver, who, by a special run of ill-luck, was always engaged by a publisher of Bonapartist works, and was busy at that moment upon a portrait of the Prince Imperial, in the uniform of a corporal of the Guards, with an immense bearskin cap upon his childish head.

Father Gerard was growing old. His beard, formerly of a reddish shade, and what little hair there was remaining upon his head, had become silvery white; that wonderful white which, like a tardy recompense to red-faced persons, becomes their full-blooded faces so well. The good man felt the weight of years, as did his wife, whose flesh increased in such a troublesome way that she was forced to pant heavily when she seated herself after climbing the five flights. Father Gerard grew old, like everything that surrounded him; like the house opposite, that he had seen built, and that no longer had the air of a new building; like his curious old furniture, his mended crockery, and his engravings, yellow with age, the frames of which had turned red; like the old Erard piano, upon which Louise, an accomplished performer, now was playing a set of Beethoven's waltzes and Mendelssohn's "Songs Without Words." This poor old servant now had only the shrill, trembling tones of a harmonica.

The poor artist grew old, and he was uneasy as to the future; for he had not known how to manage like his school-friend, the intriguing Damourette, who had formerly cheated him out of the 'prix de Rome' by a favor, and who now played the gentleman at the Institute, in his embroidered coat, and received all the good orders. He, the simpleton, had saddled himself with a family, and although he had drudged like a slave he had laid nothing aside. One day he might be stricken with apoplexy and leave his widow without resources, and his two daughters without a dowry. He sometimes thought of all this as he filled his pipe, and it was not pleasant.

If M. Gerard grew gloomy as he grew older, M. Violette became mournful. He was more than forty years old now. What a decline! Does grief make the years count double? The widower was a mere wreck. His rebellious lock of hair had become a dirty gray, and always hung over his right eye, and he no longer took the trouble to toss it behind his ear. His hands trembled and he felt his memory leaving him. He grew more taciturn and silent than ever, and seemed interested in nothing, not even in his son's studies. He returned home late, ate little at dinner, and then went out again with a tottering step to pace the dark, gloomy streets. At the office, where he still did his work mechanically, he was a doomed man; he never would be elected chief assistant. "What depravity!" said one of his fellow clerks, a young man with a bright future, protected by the head of the department, who went to the races and had not his equal in imitating the "Gnoufl gnoufl" of Grassot, the actor. "A man of his age does not decline so rapidly without good cause. It is not natural!" What is it, then, that has reduced M. Violette to such a degree of dejection and wretchedness?

Alas! we must admit it. The unhappy man lacked courage, and he sought consolation in his despair, and found it in a vice.

Every evening when he left his office he went into a filthy little cafe on the Rue du Four. He would seat himself upon a bench in the back of the room, in the darkest corner, as if ashamed; and would ask in a low tone for his first glass of absinthe. His first! Yes, for he drank two, three even. He drank them in little sips, feeling slowly rise within him the cerebral rapture of the powerful liquor. Let those who are happy blame him if they will! It was there, leaning upon the marble table, looking at, without seeing her, through the pyramids of lump sugar and bowls of punch, the lady cashier with her well oiled hair reflected in the glass behind her—it was there that the inconsolable widower found forgetfulness of his trouble. It was there that for one hour he lived over again his former happiness.

For, by a phenomenon well known to drinkers of absinthe, he regulated and governed his intoxication, and it gave him the dream that he desired.

"Boy, one glass of absinthe!"

And once more he became the young husband, who adores his dear Lucie and is adored by her.

It is winter, he is seated in the corner by the fire, and before him, sitting in the light reflected by a green lampshade upon which dark silhouettes of jockey-riders are running at full speed, his wife is busying herself with some embroidery. Every few moments they look at each other and smile, he over his book and she over her work; the lover never tired of admiring Lucie's delicate fingers. She is too pretty! Suddenly he falls at her feet, slips his arm about her waist, and gives her a long kiss; then, overcome with languor, he puts his head upon his beloved's knees and hears her say to him, in a low voice: "That is right! Go to sleep!" and her soft hands lightly stroke his hair.

"Boy, one glass of absinthe!"

They are in that beautiful field filled with flowers, near the woods in Verrieres, upon a fine June afternoon when the sun is low. She has made a magnificent bouquet of field flowers. She stops at intervals to add a cornflower, and he follows, carrying her mantle and umbrella. How beautiful is summer and how sweet it is to love! They are a little tired; for during the whole of this bright Sunday they have wandered through the meadows. It is the hour for dinner, and here is a little tavern under some lindens, where the whiteness of the napkins rivals the blossoming thickets. They choose a table and order their repast of a moustached youth. While waiting for their soup, Lucie, rosy from being out all day in the open air and silent from hunger, amuses herself in looking at the blue designs on the plates, which represented battles in Africa. What a joyous dinner! There were mushrooms in the omelet, mushrooms in the stewed kidneys, mushrooms in the filet. But so much the better! They are very fond of them. And the good wine! The dear child is almost intoxicated at dessert! She takes it into her head to squeeze a cherry-stone between her thumb and first finger and makes it pop-slap! into her husband's face! And the naughty creature laughs! But he will have his revenge—wait a little! He rises, and leaning over the table buries two fingers between her collar and her neck, and the mischievous creature draws her head down into her shoulders as far as she can, begging him, with a nervous laugh, "No, no, I beseech you!" for she is afraid of being tickled. But the best time of all is the return through the country at night, the exquisite odor of new-mown hay, the road lighted by a summer sky where the whole zodiac twinkles, and through which, like a silent stream, the Chemin de St. Jacques rolls its diamond smoke.

Tired and happy she hangs upon her husband's arm. How he loves her! It seems to him that his love for Lucie is as deep and profound as the night. "Nobody is coming let me kiss your dear mouth!" and their kisses are so pure, so sincere, and so sweet, that they ought to rejoice the stars!

"Another glass of absinthe, boy—one more!"

And the unhappy man would forget for a few moments longer that he ought to go back to his lonely lodging, where the servant had laid the table some time before, and his little son awaited him, yawning with hunger and reading a book placed beside his plate. He forgot the horrible moment of returning, when he would try to hide his intoxicated condition under a feint of bad humor, and when he would seat himself at table without even kissing Amedee, in order that the child should not smell his breath.

A ROMANCE OF YOUTH

By FRANCOIS COPPEE

BOOK 2.

CHAPTER V

AMEDEE MAKES FRIENDS

Meanwhile the allegorical old fellow with the large wings and white beard, Time, had emptied his hour-glass many times; or, to speak plainer, the postman, with a few flakes of snow upon his blue cloth coat, presents himself three or four times a day at his customers' dwelling to offer in return for a trifling sum of money a calendar containing necessary information, such as the ecclesiastical computation, or the difference between the Gregorian and the Arabic Hegira; and Amedee Violette had gradually become a young man.

A young man! that is to say, a being who possesses a treasure without knowing its value, like a Central African negro who picks up one of M. Rothschild's cheque-books; a young man ignorant of his beauty or charms, who frets because the light down upon his chin has not turned into hideous bristles, a young man who awakes every morning full of hope, and artlessly asks himself what fortunate thing will happen to him to-day; who dreams, instead of living, because he is timid and poor.

It was then that Amedee made the acquaintance of one of his comrades—he no longer went to M. Batifol's boarding-school, but was completing his studies at the Lycee Henri IV—named Maurice Roger. They soon formed an affectionate intimacy, one of those eighteen-year-old friendships which are perhaps the sweetest and most substantial in the world.

Amedee was attracted, at first sight, by Maurice's handsome, blond, curly head, his air of frankness and superiority, and the elegant jackets that he wore with the easy, graceful manners of a gentleman. Twice a day, when they left the college, they walked together through the Luxembourg Gardens, confiding to each other their dreams and hopes, lingering in the walks, where Maurice already gazed at the grisettes in an impudent fashion, talking with the charming abandon of their age, the sincere age when one thinks aloud.

Maurice told his new friend that he was the son of an officer killed before Sebastopol, that his mother had never married again, but adored him and indulged him in all his whims. He was patiently waiting for his school-days to end, to live independently in the Latin Quarter, to study law, without being hurried, since his mother wished him to do so, and he did not wish to displease her. But he wished also to amuse himself with painting, at least as an amateur; for he was passionately fond of it. All this was said by the handsome, aristocratic young man with a happy smile, which expanded his sensual lips and nostrils; and Amedee admired him without one envious thought; feeling, with the generous warmth of youth, an entire confidence in the future and the mere joy of living.

In his turn he made a confidant of Maurice, but not of everything. The poor boy could not tell anybody that he suspected his father of a secret vice, that he blushed over it, was ashamed of it, and suffered from it as much as youth can suffer. At least, honest-hearted fellow that he was, he avowed his humble origin without shame, boasted of his humble friends the Gerards, praised Louise's goodness, and spoke enthusiastically of little Maria, who was just sixteen and so pretty.

"You will take me to see them some time, will you not?" said Maurice, who listened to his friend with his natural good grace. "But first of all, you must come to dinner some day with me, and I will present you to my mother. Next Sunday, for instance. Is it agreeable?"

Amedee would have liked to refuse, for he suddenly recalled—oh! the torture and suffering of poor young men! that his Sunday coat was almost as seedy as his everyday one, that his best pair of shoes were run-over at the heels, and that the collars and cuffs on his six white shirts were ragged on the edges from too frequent washings. Then, to go to dinner in the city, what an ordeal! What must he do to be presented in a drawing-room? The very thought of it made him shiver. But Maurice invited him so cordially that he was irresistible, and Amedee accepted.

The following Sunday, then, spruced up in his best-what could have possessed the haberdasher to induce him to buy a pair of red dog-skin gloves? He soon saw that they were too new and too startling for the rest of his costume—Amedee went up to the first floor of a fine house on the Faubourg St. Honore and rang gently at the door on the left. A young and pretty maid—one of those brunettes who have a waist that one can clasp in both hands, and a suspicion of a moustache—opened the door and ushered the young man into a drawing-room furnished in a simple but luxurious manner. Maurice was alone, standing with his back to the fire, in the attitude of master of the house. He received his friend with warm demonstrations of pleasure. Amedee's eyes were at once attracted by the portrait of a handsome lieutenant of artillery, dressed in the regimental coat, with long skirts, of 1845, and wearing a sword-belt fastened by two lion's heads. This officer, in parade costume, was painted in the midst of a desert, seated under a palm-tree.

"That is my father," said Maurice. "Do I not resemble him?"

The resemblance was really striking. The same warm, pleasant smile, and even the same blond curls. Amedee was admiring it when a voice repeated behind him, like an echo:

"Maurice resembles him, does he not?"

It was Madame Roger who had quietly entered. When Amedee saw this stately lady in mourning, with a Roman profile, and clear, white complexion, who threw such an earnest glance at her son, then at her husband's portrait, Amedee comprehended that Maurice was his mother's idol, and, moved by the sight of the widow, who would have been beautiful but for her gray hair and eyelids, red from so much weeping, he stammered a few words of thanks for the invitation to dinner.

"My son has told me," said she, "that you are the one among all his comrades that he cares for most. I know what affection you have shown him. I am the one who should thank you, Monsieur Amedee."

They seated themselves and talked; every few moments these words were spoken by Madame Roger with an accent of pride and tenderness, "My son . . . . my son Maurice." Amedee realized how pleasant his friend's life must be with such a good mother, and he could not help comparing his own sad childhood, recalling above all things the lugubrious evening repasts, when, for several years now, he had buried his nose in his plate so as not to see his father's drunken eyes always fastened upon him as if to ask for his pardon.

Maurice let his mother praise him for a few moments, looking at her with a pleasant smile which became a trifle saddened. Finally he interrupted her:

"It is granted, mamma, that I am a perfect phoenix," and he gayly embraced her.

At this moment the pretty maid announced, "Monsieur and Mesdemoiselles Lantz," and Madame Roger arose hastily to receive the newcomers. Lieutenant-Colonel Lantz, of the Engineer Corps, was with Captain Roger when he died in the trench before Mamelon Vert; and might have been at that time pleasant to look upon, in his uniform with its black velvet breastplate; but, having been promoted some time ago to the office, he had grown aged, leaning over the plans and draughts on long tables covered with rules and compasses. With a cranium that looked like a picked bird, his gray, melancholy imperial, his stooping shoulders, which shortened still more his tightly buttoned military coat, there was nothing martial in his appearance. With his head full of whims, no fortune, and three daughters to marry, the poor Colonel, who put on only two or three times a year, for official solemnities, his uniform, which he kept in camphor, dined every Sunday night with Madame Roger, who liked this estimable man because he was her husband's best friend, and had invited him with his three little girls, who looked exactly alike, with their turned-up noses, florid complexions, and little, black, bead-like eyes, always so carefully dressed that one involuntarily compared them to three pretty cakes prepared for some wedding or festive occasion. They sat down at the table.

Madame Roger employed an excellent cook, and for the first time in his life Amedee ate a quantity of good things, even more exquisite than Mamma Gerard's little fried dishes. It was really only a very comfortable and nice dinner, but to the young man it was a revelation of unsuspected pleasures. This decorated table, this cloth that was so soft when he put his hand upon it; these dishes that excited and satisfied the appetite; these various flavored wines which, like the flowers, were fragrant—what new and agreeable sensations! They were quickly and silently waited upon by the pretty maid. Maurice, seated opposite his mother, presided over the repast with his elegant gayety. Madame Roger's pale face would light up with a smile at each of his good-natured jokes, and the three young ladies would burst into discreet little laughs, all in unison, and even the sorrowful Colonel would arouse from his torpor.

He became animated after his second glass of burgundy, and was very entertaining. He spoke of the Crimean campaign; of that chivalrous war when the officers of both armies, enemies to each other, exchanged politenesses and cigars during the suspension of arms. He told fine military anecdotes, and Madame Roger, seeing her son's face excited with enthusiasm at these heroic deeds, became gloomy at once. Maurice noticed it first.

"Take care, Colonel," said he. "You will frighten mamma, and she will imagine at once that I still wish to enter Saint-Cyr. But I assure you, little mother, you may be tranquil. Since you wish it, your respectful and obedient son will become a lawyer without clients, who will paint daubs during his spare moments. In reality, I should much prefer a horse and a sword and a squadron of hussars. But no matter! The essential thing is not to give mamma any trouble."

This was said with so much warmth and gentleness, that Madame Roger and the Colonel exchanged softened looks; the young ladies were also moved, as much as pastry can be, and they all fixed upon Maurice their little black eyes, which had suddenly become so soft and tender that Amedee did not doubt but that they all had a sentimental feeling for Maurice, and thought him very fortunate to have the choice between three such pretty pieces for dessert.

How all loved this charming and graceful Maurice, and how well he knew how to make himself beloved!

Later, when they served the champagne, he arose, glass in hand, and delivered a burlesque toast, finding some pleasant word for all his guests. What frank gayety! what a hearty laugh went around the table! The three young ladies giggled themselves as red as peonies. A sort of joyous chuckle escaped from the Colonel's drooping moustache. Madame Roger's smile seemed to make her grow young; and Amedee noticed, in a corner of the dining-room, the pretty maid, who restrained herself no more than the others; and when she showed her teeth, that were like a young puppy's, she was charming indeed.

After the tea the Colonel, who lived at some distance, near the Military School, and who, as the weather was fine, wished to walk home and avoid the expense of a cab, left with his three marriageable daughters, and Amedee in his turn took his departure.

In the ante-chamber, the maid said to Maurice, as she helped him on with his topcoat.

"I hope that you will not come in very late this evening, Monsieur Maurice."

"What is that, Suzanne?" replied the young man, without anger, but a trifle impatiently. "I shall return at the hour that pleases me."

As he descended the stairs ahead of Amedee, he said, with a laugh

"Upon my word! she will soon make her jealousy public."

"What!" exclaimed Amedee, glad that his companion could not see his blushes.

"Well, yes! Is she not pretty? I admit it, Violette; I have not, like you, the artlessness of the flower whose name you bear. You will have to resign yourself to it; you have a very bad fellow for a friend. As to the rest, be content. I have resolved to scandalize the family roof no longer. I have finished with this bold-faced creature. You must know that she began it, and was the first to kiss me on the sly. Now, I am engaged elsewhere. Here we are outside, and here is a carriage. Here, driver! You will allow me to bid you adieu. It is only a quarter past ten. I still have time to appear at Bullier's and meet Zoe Mirilton. Until tomorrow, Violette."

Amedee returned home very much troubled. So, then, his friend was a libertine. But he made excuses for him. Had he not just seen him so charming to his mother and so respectful to the three young ladies? Maurice had allowed himself to be carried away by his youthful impetuosity, that was all! Was it for him, still pure, but tormented by the temptations and curiosity of youth, to be severe? Would he not have done as much had he dared, or if he had had the money in his pocket? To tell the truth, Amedee dreamed that very night of the pretty maid with the suspicion of a moustache.

The next day, when Amedee paid his visit to the Gerards, all they could talk of was the evening before. Amedee spoke with the eloquence of a young man who had seen for the first time a finger-bowl at dessert.

Louise, while putting on her hat and getting her roll of music—she gave lessons now upon the piano in boarding-schools—was much interested in Madame Roger's imposing beauty. Mamma Gerard would have liked to know how the chicken-jelly was made; the old engraver listened with pleasure to the Colonel's military anecdotes; while little Maria exacted a precise description of the toilettes of the three demoiselles Lantz, and turned up her nose disdainfully at them.

"Now, then, Amedee," said the young girl, suddenly, as she looked at herself in a mirror that was covered with flyspecks, "tell me honestly, were these young ladies any prettier than I?"

"Do you see the coquette?" exclaimed Father Gerard, bursting into laughter without raising his eyes from his work. "Do people ask such questions as that, Mademoiselle?"

There was a general gayety, but Amedee blushed without knowing why. Oh! no, certainly those three young ladies in their Savoy-cake skirts and nougat waists were not as pretty as little Maria in her simple brown frock. How she improved from day to day! It seemed to Amedee as if he never had seen her before until this minute. Where had she found that supple, round waist, that mass of reddish hair which she twisted upon the top of her head, that lovely complexion, that mouth, and those eyes that smiled with the artless tenderness of young flowers?

Mamma Gerard, while laughing like the others, scolded her daughter a little for her attack of feminine vanity, and then began to talk of Madame Roger in order to change the conversation.

Amedee did not cease to praise his friend. He told how affectionate he was to his mother, how he resisted the military blood that burned in him, how graceful he was, and how, at eighteen years, he did the honor of the drawing-room and table with all the manner of a grand seigneur.

Maria listened attentively.

"You have promised to bring him here, Amedee," said the spoiled child, with a serious air. "I should like very much to see him once."

Amedee repeated his promise; but on his way to the Lycee, for his afternoon class, he recalled the incident of the pretty maid and the name of Zoe Mirilton, and, seized with some scruples, he asked himself whether he ought to introduce his friend to the young Gerard girls. At first this idea made him uneasy, then he thought that it was ridiculous. Was not Maurice a good-hearted young man and well brought up? Had he not seen him conduct himself with tact and reserve before Colonel Lantz's daughters?

Some days later Maurice reminded him of the promised visit to the Gerards, and Amedee presented him to his old friends.

Louise was not at home; she had been going about teaching for some time to increase the family's resources, for the engraver was more red-faced than ever, and obliged to change the number of his spectacles every year, and could not do as much work as formerly.

But the agreeable young man made a conquest of the rest of the family by his exquisite good-nature and cordial, easy manner. Respectful and simple with Madame Gerard, whom he intimidated a little, he paid very little attention to Maria and did not appear to notice that he was exciting her curiosity to the highest pitch. He modestly asked Father Gerard's advice upon his project of painting, amusing himself with the knickknacks about the apartments, picking out by instinct the best engravings and canvases of value. The good man was enchanted with Maurice and hastened to show him his private museum, forgetting all about his pipe—he was smoking at present a Garibaldi—and presented him his last engraving, where one saw—it certainly was a fatality that pursued the old republican!—the Emperor Napoleon III, at Magenta, motionless upon his horse in the centre of a square of grenadiers, cut down by grape and canister.

Maurice's visit was short, and as Amedee had thought a great deal about little Maria for several days, he asked his friend, as he conducted him a part of the way:

"What did you think of her?"

Maurice simply replied, "Delicious!" and changed the conversation.

CHAPTER VI

DREAMS OF LOVE

Solemn moment approached for the two friends. They were to take their examinations for graduation. Upon the days when M. Violette—they now called him at the office "Father Violette," he had grown so aged and decrepit—was not too much "consoled" in the cafe in the Rue du Four, and when he was less silent and gloomy than usual, he would say to his son, after the soup:

"Do you know, Amedee, I shall not be easy in my mind until you have received your degree. Say what they may, it leads to everything."

To everything indeed! M. Violette had a college friend upon whom all the good marks had been showered, who, having been successively schoolmaster, journalist, theatrical critic, a boarder in Mazas prison, insurance agent, director of an athletic ring—he quoted Homer in his harangue—at present pushed back the curtains at the entrance to the Ambigu, and waited for his soup at the barracks gate, holding out an old tomato-can to be filled.

But M. Violette had no cause to fear! Amedee received his degree on the same day with his friend Maurice, and both passed honorably. A little old man with a head like a baboon—the scientific examiner—tried to make Amedee flounder on the subject of nitrogen, but he passed all the same. One can hope for everything nowadays.

But what could Amedee hope for first? M. Violette thought of it when he was not at his station at the Rue du Four. What could he hope for? Nothing very great.

Probably he could enter the ministry as an auxiliary. One hundred francs a month, and the gratuities, would not be bad for a beginner! M. Violette recalled his endless years in the office, and all the trouble he had taken to guess a famous rebus that was celebrated for never having been solved. Was Amedee to spend his youth deciphering enigmas? M. Violette hoped for a more independent career for his son, if it were possible. Commerce, for example! Yes! there was a future in commerce. As a proof of it there was the grocer opposite him, a simpleton who probably did not put the screws on enough and had just hanged himself rather than go into bankruptcy. M. Violette would gladly see his son in business. If he could begin with M. Gaufre? Why not? The young man might become in the end his uncle's partner and make his fortune. M. Violette spoke of it to Amedee.

"Shall we go to see your uncle Sunday morning?"

The idea of selling chasubles and Stations of the Cross did not greatly please Amedee, who had concealed in his drawer a little book full of sonnets, and had in his mind the plan of a romantic drama wherein one would say "Good heavens!" and "My lord!" But first of all, he must please his father. He was glad to observe that for some time M. Violette had interested himself more in him, and had resisted his baneful habit somewhat. The young man offered no resistance. The next day at noon he presented himself at the Rue Servandoni, accompanied by his father.

The "dealer in pious goods" received them with great good-humor. He had just come from high mass and was about to sit down at the table. He even invited them to follow his example and taste of his stewed kidneys, one of Berenice's triumphs, who served the dinner with her hands loaded with rings. The Violettes had dined, and the father made known his desire.

"Yes," said Uncle Isidore, "Amedee might enter the house. Only you know, Violette, it will be another education to be learned over again. He must begin at the very beginning and follow the regular course. Oh! the boy will not be badly treated! He may take his meals with us, is not that so, Berenice? At first he would be obliged to run about a little, as I did when I came from the province to work in the shop and tie up parcels."

M. Violette looked at his son and saw that he was blushing with shame. The poor man understood his mistake. What good to have dazzled M. Patin before the whole University by reciting, without hesitation, three verses of Aristophanes, only to become a drudge and a packer? Well! so Amedee would yawn over green boxes and guess at enigmas in the Illustration. It had to be so.

They took leave of Uncle Isidore.

"We will reflect over it, Monsieur Gaufre, and will come to see you again."

But Berenice had hardly shut the door upon them when M. Violette said to his son:

"Nothing is to be expected of that old egotist. Tomorrow we will go to see the chief of my department, I have spoken of you to him, at all events."

He was a good sort of fellow, this M. Courtet, who was head clerk, though too conceited and starched up, certainly. His red rosette, as large as a fifty-cent piece, made one's eyes blink, and he certainly was very imprudent to stand so long backed up to the fireplace with limbs spread apart, for it seemed that he must surely burn the seat of his trousers. But no matter, he has stomach enough. He has noticed M. Violette's pitiful decline—"a poor devil who never will live to be promoted." Having it in his power to distribute positions, M. Courtet had reserved a position for Amedee. In eight days the young man would be nominated an auxiliary employe at fifteen hundred francs a year. It is promised and done.

Ugh! the sickening heat from the stove! the disgusting odor of musty papers! However, Amedee had nothing to complain of; they might have given him figures to balance for five hours at a time. He owed it to M. Courtet's kindness, that he was put at once into the correspondence room. He studied the formulas, and soon became skilful in official politeness. He now knew the delicate shades which exist between "yours respectfully" and "most respectfully yours;" and he measured the abyss which separates an "agreeable" and "homage."

To sum it all up, Amedee was bored, but he was not unhappy; for he had time to dream.

He went the longest way to the office in the morning, while seeking to make "amour" rhyme with "jour" without producing an insipid thing; or else he thought of the third act of his drama after the style of 1830, and the grand love scene which should take place at the foot of the Montfaucon gallows. In the evening he went to the Gerards, and they seated themselves around—the lamp which stood on the dining-room table, the father reading his journal, the women sewing. He chatted with Maria, who answered him the greater part of the time without raising her eyes, because she suspected, the coquette! that he admired her beautiful, drooping lids.

Amedee composed his first sonnets in her honor, and he adored her, of course, but he was also in love with the Lantz young ladies, whom he saw sometimes at Madame Roger's, and who each wore Sunday evenings roses in her hair, which made them resemble those pantheons in sponge-cake that pastry-cooks put in their windows on fete days.

If Amedee had been presented to twelve thousand maidens successively, they would have inspired twelve thousand wishes. There was the servant of the family on the first floor, whose side-glance troubled him as he met her on the staircase; and his heart sank every time he turned the handle of the door of a shop in the Rue Bonaparte, where an insidious clerk always forced him to choose ox-colored kid gloves, which he detested. It must not be forgotten that Amedee was very young, and was in love with love.

He was so extremely timid that he never had had the audacity to tell the girl at the glove counter that he preferred bronze-green gloves, nor the boldness to show Maria Gerard his poems composed in her honor, in which he now always put the plural "amours," so as to make it rhyme with "toujours," which was an improvement. He never had dared to reply to the glance of the little maid on the second floor; and he was very wrong to be embarrassed, for one morning, as he passed the butcher's shop, he saw the butcher's foreman put his arm about the girl's waist and whisper a love speech over a fine sirloin roast.

Sometimes, in going or coming from the office, Amedee would go to see his friend Maurice, who had obtained from Madame Roger permission to install himself in the Latin Quarter so as to be near the law school.

In a very low-studded first-floor room in the Rue Monsieur-le-Prince, Amedee perceived through a cloud of tobacco-smoke the elegant Maurice in a scarlet jacket lying upon a large divan. Everything was rich and voluptuous, heavy carpets, handsomely bound volumes of poems, an open piano, and an odor of perfumery mingled with that of cigarettes. Upon the velvet-covered mantel Mademoiselle Irma, the favorite of the master of the apartment, had left the last fashionable novel, marking, with one of her hairpins, where she had left off reading. Amedee spent a delightful hour there. Maurice always greeted him with his joyful, kind manner, in which one hardly minded the slight shade of patronage. He walked up and down his room, expanding his finely moulded chest, lighting and throwing away his cigarettes, seating himself for two minutes at the piano and playing one of Chopin's sad strains, opening a book and reading a page, showing his albums to his friend, making him repeat some of his poems, applauding him and touching lightly upon different subjects, and charming Amedee more and more by his grace and manners.

However, Amedee could not enjoy his friend much, as he rarely found him alone. Every few moments—the key was in the door—Maurice's comrades, young pleasure-seekers like himself, but more vulgar, not having his gentlemanly bearing and manners, would come to talk with him of some projected scheme or to remind him of some appointment for the evening.

Often, some one of them, with his hat upon his head, would dash off a polka, after placing his lighted cigar upon the edge of the piano. These fast fellows frightened Amedee a little, as he had the misfortune to be fastidious.

After these visitors had left, Maurice would ask his friend to dinner, but the door would open again, and Mademoiselle Irma, in her furs and small veil—a comical little face—would enter quickly and throw her arms about Amedee's neck, kissing him, while rumpling his hair with her gloved hands.

"Bravo! we will all three dine together."

No! Amedee is afraid of Mademoiselle Irma, who has already thrown her mantle upon the sofa and crowned the bronze Venus de Milo with her otter toque. The young man excuses himself, he is expected at home.

"Timid fellow, go!" said Maurice to him, as he conducted him to the door, laughing.

What longings! What dreams! They made up all of poor Amedee's life. Sometimes they were sad, for he suffered in seeing his father indulge himself more and more in his vice. No woman loved him, and he never had one louis in his pocket for pleasure or liberty. But he did not complain. His life was noble and happy! He smiled with pleasure as he thought of his good friends; his heart beat in great throbs as he thought of love; he wept with rapture over beautiful verses. The spectacle of life, through hope and the ideal, seemed to him transfigured. Happy Amedee! He was not yet twenty years old!

CHAPTER VII

A GENTLE COUNSELLOR

One sombre, misty, winter morning, as Amedee lingered in his bed, his father entered, bringing him a letter that the wife of the concierge had just brought up. The letter was from Maurice, inviting his friend to dinner that evening at seven o'clock at Foyots, to meet some of his former companions at the Lycee Henri IV.

"Will you excuse me for not dining with you this evening, papa?" said Amedee, joyfully. "Maurice Roger entertains us at a restaurant."

The young man's gayety left him suddenly when he looked at his father, who had seated himself on the side of the bed. He had become almost frightful to look at; old before his time, livid of complexion, his eyes bloodshot, the rebellious lock of hair straggling over his right temple. Nothing was more heartbreaking than his senile smile when he placed his bony trembling hands upon his thighs. Amedee, who knew, alas, why his father had reached such a pass, felt his heart moved with pity and shame.

"Are you suffering to-day?" asked the young man. "Would you prefer that we should dine together as usual? I will send word to Maurice. Nothing is easier."

"No, my child, no!" replied M. Violette, in a hollow tone. "Go and amuse yourself with your friends. I know perfectly well that the life you lead with me is too monotonous. Go and amuse yourself, it will please me—only there is an idea that troubles me more than usual—and I want to confide it to you."

"What is it then, dear papa?"

"Amedee, last March your mother had been dead fifteen years. You hardly knew her. She was the sweetest and best of creatures, and all that I can wish you is, that you may meet such a woman, make her your companion for life, and be more fortunate than I, my poor Amedee, and keep her always. During these frightful years since your mother's death I have suffered, do you see? suffered horribly, and I have never, never been consoled. If I have lived—if I have had the strength to live, in spite of all, it was only for you and in remembrance of her. I think I have nearly finished my task. You are a young man, intelligent and honest, and you have now an employment which will give you your bread. However, I often ask myself—oh, very often—whether I have fulfilled my duty toward you. Ah! do not protest," added the unhappy man, whom Amedee had clasped in his arms. "No, my poor child, I have not loved you sufficiently; grief has filled too large a place in my heart; above all, during these last few years I have not been with you enough. I have sought solitude. You understand me, Amedee, I can not tell you more," he said, with a sob. "There are some parts of my life that you must ignore, and if it grieves you to know what I have become during that time, you must never think of it; forget it. I beg of you, my child, do not judge me severely. And one of these days, if I die-ah! we must expect it—the burden of my grief is too heavy for me to bear, it crushes me! Well, my child, if I die, promise me to be indulgent to my memory, and when you think of your father only say: 'He was very unhappy!'"

Amedee shed tears upon his father's shoulder, who softly stroked his son's beautiful hair with his trembling hands.

"My father, my good father!" sobbed Amedee, "I love and respect you with all my heart. I will dress myself quickly and we will go to the office together; we will return the same way and dine like a pair of good friends. I beg of you, do not ask me to leave you to-day!"

But M. Violette suddenly arose as if he had formed some resolution.

"No, Amedee," said he, firmly. "I have said what I had to say to you, and you will remember it. That is sufficient. Go and amuse yourself this evening with your friends. Sadness is dangerous at your age. As for myself, I shall go to dine with Pere Bastide, who has just received his pension, and has invited me more than twenty times to come and see his little house at Grand Montrouge. It is understood; I wish it. Now then, wipe your eyes and kiss me."

Having tenderly embraced his son, M. Violette left the room. Amedee could hear him in the vestibule take down his hat and cane, open and close the door, and go down the stairs with a heavy step. A quarter of an hour after, as the young man was crossing the Luxembourg to go to the office, he met Louise Gerard with her roll of music in her hand, going to give some lessons in the city. He walked a few steps beside her, and the worthy girl noticed his red eyes and disturbed countenance.

"What is the matter with you, Amedee?" she inquired, anxiously.

"Louise," he replied, "do you not think that my father has changed very much in the last few months?"

She stopped and looked at him with eyes shining with compassion.

"Very much changed, my poor Amedee. You would not believe me if I told you that I had not remarked it. But whatever may be the cause—how shall I say it?—that has affected your father's health, you should think of only one thing, my friend; that is, that he has been tender and devoted to you; that he became a widower very young and he did not remarry; that he has endured, in order to devote himself to his only child, long years of solitude and unhappy memories. You must think of that, Amedee, and that only."

"I never shall forget it, Louise, never fear; my heart is full of gratitude. This morning, even, he was so affectionate and kind to me—but his health is ruined; he is now a weak old man. Soon—I not only fear it, but I am certain of it—soon he will be incapable of work. I can see his poor hands tremble now. He will not even have a right to a pension. If he could not continue to work in the office he could hardly obtain a meagre relief, and that by favor only. And for long years I can only hope for an insufficient salary. Oh! to think that the catastrophe draws near, that one of these days he may fall ill and become infirm, perhaps, and that we shall be almost needy and I shall be unable to surround him with care in his old age. That is what makes me tremble!"

They walked along side by side upon the moist, soft ground of the large garden, under the leafless trees, where hung a slight penetrating mist which made them shiver under their wraps.

"Amedee," said she, looking at the young man with a serious gentleness, "I have known you from a child, and I am the elder. I am twenty-two; that makes me almost an old maid, Amedee, and gives me the right to scold you a little. You lack confidence in life, my friend, and it is wrong at your age. Do you think I do not see that my father has aged very much, that his eyesight fails, that we are much more cramped in circumstances in the house than formerly? Are we any the more sad? Mamma makes fewer little dishes and I teach in Paris, that is all. We live nearly the same as before, and our dear Maria—she is the pet of us all, the joy and pride of the house-well, our Maria, all the same, has from time to time a new frock or a pretty hat. I have no experience, but it seems to me that in order to feel really unhappy I must have nobody to love—that is the only privation worth the trouble of noticing. Do you know that I have just had one of the greatest pleasures of my life? I noticed that papa did not smoke as much as usual, in order to be economical, poor man! Fortunately I found a new pupil at Batignolles, and as soon as I had the first month's pay in my pocket I bought a large package of tobacco and put it beside his work. One must never complain so long as one is fortunate enough to keep those one loves. I know the secret grief that troubles you regarding your father; but think what he has suffered, that he loves you, that you are his only consolation. And when you have gloomy thoughts, come and see your old friends, Amedee. They will try to warm your heart at the fireside of their friendship, and to give you some of their courage, the courage of poor people which is composed of a little indifference and a little resignation."

They had reached the Florentine Terrace, where stand the marble statues of queens and ladies, and on the other side of the balustrade, ornamented with large vases, they could see through the mist the reservoir with its two swans, the solitary gravel walks, the empty grass-plots of a pale green, surrounded by the skeletons of lilac-trees, and the facade of the old palace, whose clock-hands pointed to ten.

"Let us hasten," said Louise, after a glance at the dial. "Escort me as far at the Odeon omnibus. I am a little late."

As he walked by her side he looked at her. Alas! Poor Louise was not pretty, in spite of her large eyes, so loving but not coquettish. She wore a close, ugly hat, a mantle drawn tightly about her shoulders, colored gloves, and heavy walking-shoes. Yes, she was a perfect picture of a "two francs an hour" music-teacher. What a good, brave girl! With what an overflowing heart she had spoken of her family! It was to earn tobacco for her father and a new frock for her pretty sister that she left thus, so early in the misty morning, and rode in public conveyances, or tramped through the streets of Paris in the mud. The sight of her, more than what she said, gave the weak and melancholy Amedee courage and desire for manly resolutions.

"My dear Louise," said he, with emotion, "I am very fortunate to have such a friend as you, and for so many years! Do you remember when we used to have our hunts after the bearskin cap when we were children?"

They had just left the garden and found themselves behind the Odeon. Two tired-out omnibus horses, of a yellowish-white, and showing their ribs, were rubbing their noses against each other like a caress; then the horse on the left raised his head and placed it in a friendly way upon the other's mane. Louise pointed to the two animals and said to Amedee, smilingly:

"Their fate is hard, is it not? No matter! they are good friends, and that is enough to help them endure it."

Then, shaking hands with Amedee, she climbed lightly up into the carriage.

All that day at the office Amedee was uneasy about his father, and about four o'clock, a little before the time for his departure, he went to M. Violette's office. There they told him that his father had just left, saying that he would dine at Grand Montrouge with an old friend; and Amedee, a trifle reassured, decided to rejoin his friend Maurice at the Foyot restaurant.

CHAPTER VIII

BUTTERFLIES AND GRASSHOPPERS

Amedee was the first to arrive at the rendezvous. He had hardly pronounced Maurice Roger's name when a voice like a cannon bellowed out, "Now then! the yellow parlor!" and he was conducted into a room where a dazzling table was laid by a young man, with a Yankee goatee and whiskers, and the agility of a prestidigitateur. This frisky person relieved Amedee at once of his hat and coat, and left him alone in the room, radiant with lighted candles.

Evidently it was to be a banquet. Piled up in the centre of the table was a large dish of crayfish, and at each plate—there were five—were groups of large and small glasses.

Maurice came in almost immediately, accompanied by his other guests, three young men dressed in the latest fashion, whom Amedee did not at first recognize as his former comrades, who once wore wrinkled stockings and seedy coats, and wore out with him the seats of their trousers on the benches of the Lycee Henri IV.

After the greetings, "What! is it you?" "Do you remember me?" and a shaking of hands, they all seated themselves around the table.

What! is that little dumpy fellow with the turned-up nose, straight as an arrow and with such a satisfied air, Gorju, who wanted to be an actor? He is one now, or nearly so, since he studies with Regnier at the Conservatoire. A make-believe actor, he puts on airs, and in the three minutes that he has been in the room he has looked at his retrousse nose and his coarse face, made to be seen from a distance, ten times in the mirror. His first care is to inform Amedee that he has renounced his name Gorju, which was an impossible one for the theatre, and has taken that of Jocquelet. Then, without losing a moment, he refers to his "talents," "charms," and "physique."

Who is this handsome fellow with such neat side-whiskers, whose finely cut features suggest an intaglio head, and who has just placed a lawyer's heavy portfolio upon the sofa? It is Arthur Papillon, the distinguished Latin scholar who wished to organize a debating society at the Lycee, and to divide the rhetoric class into groups and sub-groups like a parliament. "What have you been doing, Papillon?" Papillon had studied law, and was secretary of the Patru Conference, of course.

Amedee immediately recognized the third guest.

"What! Gustave!" exclaimed he, joyously.

Yes! Gustave, the former "dunce," the one they had called "Good-luck" because his father had made an immense fortune in guano. Not one bit changed was Gustave! The same deep-set eyes and greenish complexion. But what style! English from the tips of his pointed shoes to the horseshoe scarfpin in his necktie. One would say that he was a horse-jockey dressed in his Sunday best. What was this comical Gustave doing now? Nothing. His father has made two hundred thousand pounds' income dabbling in certain things, and Gustave is getting acquainted with that is all—which means to wake up every morning toward noon, with a bitter mouth caused from the last night's supper, and to be surprised every morning at dawn at the baccarat table, after spending five hours saying "Bac!" in a stifled, hollow voice. Gustave understands life, and, taking into consideration his countenance like a death's-head, it may lead him to make the acquaintance of something entirely different. But who thinks of death at his age? Gustave wishes to know life, and when a fit of coughing interrupts him in one of his idiotic bursts of laughter, his comrades at the Gateux Club tell him that he has swallowed the wrong way. Wretched Gustave, so be it!

Meanwhile the boy with the juggler's motions appeared with the soup, and made exactly the same gestures when he uncovered the tureen as Robert Houdin would have made, and one was surprised not to see a bunch of flowers or a live rabbit fly out. But no! it was simply soup, and the guests attacked it vigorously and in silence. After the Rhine wine all tongues were unloosened, and as soon as they had eaten the Normandy sole-oh! what glorious appetites at twenty years of age!—the five young men all talked at once. What a racket! Exclamations crossed one another like rockets. Gustave, forcing his weak voice, boasted of the performances of a "stepper" that he had tried that morning in the Allee des Cavaliers. He would have been much better off had he stayed in his bed and taken cod-liver oil. Maurice called out to the boy to uncork the Chateau-Leoville. Amedee, having spoken of his drama to the comedian Gorju, called Jocquelet, that person, speaking in his bugle-like voice that came through his bugle-shaped nose, set himself up at once as a man of experience, giving his advice, and quoting, with admiration, Talma's famous speech to a dramatic poet: "Above all, no fine verses!" Arthur Papillon, who was destined for the courts, thought it an excellent time to lord it over the tumult of the assembly himself, and bleated out a speech of Jules Favre that he had heard the night before in the legislative assembly.

The timid Amedee was defeated at the start in this melee of conversation. Maurice also kept silent, with a slightly disdainful smile under his golden moustache, and an attack of coughing soon disabled Gustave. Alone, like two ships in line who let out, turn by turn, their volleys, the lawyer and the actor continued their cannonading. Arthur Papillon, who belonged to the Liberal opposition and wished that the Imperial government should come around to "a pacific and regular movement of parliamentary institutions," was listened to for a time, and explained, in a clear, full voice the last article in the 'Courrier du Dimanche'. But, bursting out in his terrible voice, which seemed like all of Gideon's trumpets blowing at once, the comedian took up the offensive, and victoriously declared a hundred foolish things—saying, for example, that the part of Alceste should be made a comic one; making fun of Shakespeare and Hugo, exalting Scribe, and in spite of his profile and hooked nose, which should have opened the doors of the Theatre-Francais and given him an equal share for life in its benefits, he affirmed that he intended to play lovers' parts, and that he meant to assume the responsibility of making "sympathetic" the role of Nero, in Britannicus.

This would have become terribly tiresome, but for the entrance upon the scene of some truffled partridges, which the juggler carved and distributed in less time than it would take to shuffle a pack of cards. He even served the very worst part of the bird to the simple Amedee, as he would force him to choose the nine of spades. Then he poured out the chambertin, and once more all heads became excited, and the conversation fell, as was inevitable, upon the subject of women.

Jocquelet began it, by speaking the name of one of the prettiest actresses in Paris. He knew them all and described them exactly, detailing their beauties like a slave-dealer.

"So little Lucille Prunelle is a friend of the great Moncontour—"

"Pardon me," interrupted Gustave, who was looking badly, "she has already left him for Cerfbeer the banker."

"I say she has not."

"I say that she has."

They would have quarrelled if Maurice, with his affable, bantering air, had not attacked Arthur Papillon on the subject of his love-affairs; for the young advocate drank many cups of Orleanist tea, going even into the same drawing-rooms as Beule and Prevost-Paradol, and accompanying political ladies to the receptions at the Academie Francaise.

"That is where you must make havoc, you rascal!"

But Papillon defends himself with conceited smiles and meaning looks. According to him—and he puts his two thumbs into the armholes of his vest—the ambitious must be chaste.

"Abstineo venere," said he, lowering his eyes in a comical manner, for he did not fear Latin quotations. However, he declared himself very hard to please in that matter; he dreamed of an Egeria, a superior mind. What he did not tell them was, that a dressmaker's little errand-girl, with whom he had tried to converse as he left the law-school, had surveyed him from head to foot and threatened him with the police.

Upon some new joke of Maurice's, the lawyer gave his amorous programme in the following terms:

"Understand me, a woman must be as intelligent as Hypatia, and have the sensibility of Heloise; the smile of a Joconde, and the limbs of an Antiope; and, even then, if she had not the throat of a Venus de Medicis, I should not love her."

Without going quite so far, the actor showed himself none the less exacting. According to his ideas, Deborah, the tragedienne at the Odeon—a Greek statue!—had too large hands, and the fascinating Blanche Pompon at the Varietes was a mere wax doll.

Gustave, after all, was the one who is most intractable; excited by the Bordeaux wine—a glass of mineral water would be best for him—he proclaimed that the most beautiful creature was agreeable to him only for one day; that it was a matter of principle, and that he had never made but one exception, in favor of the illustrious dancer at the Casino Cadet, Nina l'Auvergnate, because she was so comical! "Oh! my friends, she is so droll, she is enough to kill one!"

"To kill one!" Yes! my dear Monsieur Gustave, that is what will happen to you one of these fine mornings, if you do not decide to lead a more reasonable life—and on the condition that you pass your winters in the South, also!

Poor Amedee was in torture; all his illusions—desires and sentiments blended—were cruelly wounded. Then, he had just discovered a deplorable faculty; a new cause for being unhappy. The sight of this foolishness made him suffer. How these coarse young men lied! Gustave seemed to him a genuine idiot, Arthur Papillon a pedant, and as to Jocquelet, he was as unbearable as a large fly buzzing between the glass and the curtain of a nervous man's room. Fortunately, Maurice made a little diversion by bursting into a laugh.

"Well, my friends, you are all simpletons," he exclaimed. "I am not like you, thank fortune! I do not sputter over my soup. Long life to women! Yes, all of them, pretty and otherwise! For, upon my word, there are no ugly ones. I do not notice that Miss Keepsake has feet like the English, and I forget the barmaid's ruddy complexion, if she is attractive otherwise. Now do not talk in this stupid fashion, but do as I do; nibble all the apples while you have teeth. Do you know the reason why, at the moment that I am talking to the lady of the house, I notice the nose of the pretty waitress who brings in a letter on a salver? Do you know the reason why, just as I am leaving Cydalize's house, who has put a rose in my buttonhole, that I turn my head at the passing of Margoton, who is returning from the market with a basket upon her arm? It is because it is one other of my children. One other! that is a great word! Yes, one thousand and three. Don Juan was right. I feel his blood coursing in my veins. And now the boy shall uncork some champagne, shall he not? to drink to the health of love!"

Maurice was cynical, but this exposition of his philosophy served a good purpose all the same. Everybody applauded him. The prestidigitateur, who moved about the table like a schoolboy in a monkey-house, drew the cork from a bottle of Roederer—it was astonishing that fireworks did not dart out of it—and good-humor was restored. It reigned noisily until the end of the repast, when the effect was spoiled by that fool of a Gustave. He insisted upon drinking three glasses of kummel—why had they not poured in maple sirup?—and, imagining that Jocquelet looked at him askance, he suddenly manifested the intention of cutting his head open with the carafe. The comedian, who was very pale, recalled all the scenes of provocation that he had seen in the theatre; he stiffened in his chair, swelled out his chest, and stammered, "At your orders!" trying to "play the situation." But it was useless.

Gustave, restrained by Maurice and Amedee, and as drunk as a Pole, responded to his friend's objurgations by a torrent of tears, and fell under the table, breaking some of the dishes.

"Now, then, we must take the baby home," said Maurice, signing to the boy. In the twinkling of an eye the human rag called Gustave was lifted into a chair, clothed in his topcoat and hat, dressed and spruced up, pushed down the spiral staircase, and landed in a cab. Then the prestidigitateur returned and performed his last trick by making the plate disappear upon which Maurice had thrown some money to pay the bill.

It was not far from eleven o'clock when the comrades shook hands, in a thick fog, in which the gaslights looked like the orange pedlers' paper lanterns. Ugh! how damp it was!

"Good-by."

"I will see you again soon."

"Good-night to the ladies."

Arthur Papillon was in evening dress and white cravat, his customary attire every evening, and still had time to show himself in a political salon on the left side, where he met Moichod, the author of that famous Histoire de Napoleon, in which he proves that Napoleon was only a mediocre general, and that all his battles were gained by his lieutenants. Jocquelet wished to go to the Odeon and hear, for the tenth time, the fifth act of a piece of the common-sense school, in which the hero, after haranguing against money for four acts in badly rhymed verse, ends by marrying the young heiress, to the great satisfaction of the bourgeois. As to Maurice, before he went to rejoin Mademoiselle Irma at the Rue Monsieur-le-Prince, he walked part of the way with Amedee.

"These comrades of ours are a little stupid, aren't they?" said he to his friend.

"I must say that they almost disgust me," replied the young man. "Their brutal way of speaking of women and love wounded me, and you too, Maurice. So much the worse! I will be honest; you, who are so refined and proud, tell me that you did not mean what you said—that you made a pretence of vice just to please the others. It is not possible that you are content simply to gratify your appetite and make yourself a slave to your passions. You ought to have a higher ideal. Your conscience must reproach you."

Maurice brusquely interrupted this tirade, laughing in advance at what he was about to say.

"My conscience? Oh, tender and artless Violette; Oh, modest wood-flower! Conscience, my poor friend, is like a Suede glove, you can wear it soiled. Adieu! We will talk of this another day, when Mademoiselle Irma is not waiting for me."

Amedee walked on alone, shivering in the mist, weary and sad, to the Rue Notre-Dame-des-Champs.

No! it could not be true. There must be another love than that known to these brutes. There were other women besides the light creatures they had spoken of. His thoughts reverted to the companion of his childhood, to the pretty little Maria, and again he sees her sewing near the family lamp, and talking with him without raising her eyes, while he admires her beautiful, drooping lashes. He is amazed to think that this delicious child's presence has never given him the slightest uneasiness; that he has never thought of any other happiness than that of being near her. Why should not a love like that he has dreamed of some day spring up in her own heart? Have they not grown up together? Is he not the only young man that she knows intimately? What happiness to become her fiancee! Yes, it was thus that one should love! Hereafter he would flee from all temptations; he would pass all his evenings with the Gerards; he would keep as near as possible to his dear Maria, content to hear her speak, to see her smile; and he would wait with a heart full of tenderness for the moment when she would consent to become his wife. Oh! the exquisite union of two chaste beings! the adorable kiss of two innocent mouths! Did such happiness really exist?

This beautiful dream warmed the young man's heart, and he reached his home joyous and happy. He gave a vigorous pull to the bell, climbed quickly up the long flights of stairs and opened the door to their apartment. But what was this? His father must have come home very late, for a stream of light shines under the door of his sleeping-room.

"Poor man!" thought Amedee, recalling the scene of the morning. "He may be ill. Let us see."

He had hardly opened the door, when he drew back uttering a shriek of horror and distress. By the light of a candle that burned upon the mantel, Amedee had caught sight of his father extended upon the floor, his shirt disordered and covered with blood, holding in his clenched right hand the razor with which he had cut his throat.

Yes! the union of two loving hearts had at last taken place. Their love was happiness on earth; but if one of the two dies the other can never be consoled while life lasts.

M. Violette never was consoled.

CHAPTER IX

THORNS OF JEALOUSY

Now Amedee had no family. The day after his father's death he had a violent rupture with M. Isidore Gaufre. Under the pretext that a suicide horrified him, he allowed his niece's husband to be carried to the cemetery in a sixth-class hearse, and did not honor with his presence the funeral, which was even prohibited from using the parish road. But the saintly man was not deterred from swallowing for his dinner that same day, while thundering against the progress of materialism, tripe cooked after the Caen fashion, one of Berenice's weekly works of art.

Amedee had now no family, and his friends were dispersed. As a reward for passing his examinations in law, Madame Roger took her son with her on a trip to Italy, and they had just left France together.

As to the poor Gerards, just one month after M. Violette's death, the old engraver died suddenly, of apoplexy, at his work; and on that day there were not fifty francs in the house. Around the open grave where they lowered the obscure and honest artist, there was only a group of three women, in black, who were weeping, and Amedee in mourning for his father, with a dozen of Gerard's old comrades, whose romantic heads had become gray. The family was obliged to sell at once, in order to get a little money, what remained of proof-sheets in the boxes, some small paintings, old presents from artist friends who had become celebrated, and the last of the ruined knickknacks—indeed, all that constituted the charm of the house. Then, in order that her eldest daughter might not be so far from the boarding-school where she was employed as teacher of music, Madame Gerard went to live in the Rue St.-Pierre, in Montmartre, where they found a little cheap, first-floor apartment, with a garden as large as one's hand.

Now that he was reduced to his one hundred and twenty-five francs, Amedee was obliged to leave his too expensive apartment in the Rue Notre-Dame-des-Champs, and to sell the greater part of his family furniture. He kept only his books and enough to furnish his little room, perched under the roof of an old house in the Faubourg St.-Jacques.

It was far from Montmartre, so he could not see his friends as often as he would have liked, those friends whom grief in common had made dearer than ever to him. One single consolation remained for him—literary work. He threw himself into it blindly, deadening his sorrow with the fruitful and wonderful opiate of poetry and dreams. However, he had now begun to make headway, feeling that he had some thing new to say. He had long ago thrown into the fire his first poems, awkward imitations of favorite authors, also his drama after the style of 1830, where the two lovers sang a duet at the foot of the scaffold. He returned to truth and simplicity by the longest way, the schoolboy's road. Taste and inclination both induced him to express simply and honestly what he saw before him; to express, so far as he could, the humble ideal of the poor people with whom he had lived in the melancholy Parisian suburbs where his infancy was passed; in a word, to paint from nature. He tried, feeling that he could succeed; and in those days lived the most beautiful and perfect hours of his life—those in which the artist, already master of his instrument, having still the abundance and vivacity of youthful sensations, writes the first words that he knows to be good, and writes them with entire disinterestedness, not even thinking that others will see them; working for himself alone and for the sole joy of putting in visible form and spreading abroad his ideas, his thoughts-all his heart. Those moments of pure enthusiasm and perfect happiness he never could know again, even after he had nibbled at the savory food of success and had experienced the feverish desire for glory. Delicious hours they were, and sacred, too, such as can only be compared to the divine intoxication of first love.

Amedee worked courageously during the winter months that followed his father's death. He arose at six o'clock in the morning, lighted his lamp and the little stove which heated his room, and, walking up and down, leaning over his page, the poet would vigorously begin his struggle with fancies, ideas, and words. At nine o'clock he would go out and breakfast at a neighboring creamery; after which he would go to his office. There, his tiresome papers once written, he had two or three hours of leisure, which he employed in reading and taking notes from the volumes borrowed by him every morning at a reading-room on the Rue Rorer-Collard; for he had already learned that one leaves college almost ignorant, having, at best, only learned how to study. He left the office at nightfall and reached his room through the Boulevard des Invalides, and Montparnasse, which at this time was still planted with venerable elms; sometimes the lamplighter would be ahead of him, making the large gas-jets shoot out under the leafless old trees. This walk, that Amedee imposed upon himself for health's sake, would bring him, about six o'clock, a workman's appetite for his dinner,—in the little creamery situated in front of Val-de-Grace, where he had formed the habit of going. Then he would return to his garret, and relight his stove and lamp, and work until midnight. This ardent, continuous effort, this will-tension kept in his mind the warmth, animation, and excitement indispensable for poetical production. His mind expanded rapidly, ready to receive the germs that were blown to him by the mysterious winds of inspiration. At times he was astonished to see his pen fill the sheet so rapidly that he would stop, filled with pride at having thus reduced to obedience words and rhythms, and would ask himself what supernatural power had permitted him to arm these divine wild birds.

On Sundays, he had his meals brought him by the concierge, working all day and not going out until nearly five o'clock in the afternoon, to dine with Mamma Gerard. It was the only distraction that he allowed himself, or rather the only recompense that he permitted himself. He walked halfway across Paris to buy a cake in the Rue Fontaine for their dessert; then he climbed without fatigue, thanks to his young legs, to the top of Montmartre, lighted by swinging lamps, where one could almost believe one's self in the distant corner of some province. They would be waiting for him to serve the soup, and the young man would seat himself between the widow and the two orphans.

Alas, how hard these poor ladies' lives had become! Damourette, a member of the Institute, remembered that he had once joked in the studios with Gerard, and obtained a small annual pension for the widow; but it was charity—hardly enough to pay the rent. Fortunately Louise, who already looked like an old maid at twenty-three, going about the city all day with her roll of music under her black shawl, had many pupils, and more than twenty houses had well-nigh become uninhabitable through her exertions with little girls, whose red hands made an unendurable racket with their chromatic scales. Louise's earnings constituted the surest part of their revenue. What a strange paradox is the social life in large cities, where Weber's Last Waltz will bring the price of a four-pound loaf of bread, and one pays the grocer with the proceeds of Boccherini's Minuet!

In spite of all, they had hard work to make both ends meet at the Gerards. The pretty Maria wished to make herself useful and aid her mother and sister. She had always shown great taste for drawing, and her father used to give her lessons in pastel. Now she went to the Louvre to work, and tried to copy the Chardins and Latours. She went there alone. It was a little imprudent, she was so pretty; but Louise had no time to go with her, and her mother had to be at home to attend to the housework and cooking. Maria's appearance had already excited the hearts of several young daubers. There were several cases of persistent sadness and loss of appetite in Flandrin's studio; and two of Signol's pupils, who were surprised hovering about the young artist, were hated secretly as rivals; certain projects of duels, after the American fashion, were profoundly considered. To say that Maria was not a little flattered to see all these admirers turn timidly and respectfully toward her; to pretend that she took off her hat and hung it on one corner of her easel because the heat from the furnace gave her neuralgia and not to show her beautiful hair, would be as much of a lie as a politician's promise. However, the little darling was very serious, or at least tried to be. She worked conscientiously and made some progress. Her last copy of the portrait of that Marquise who holds a pug dog in her lap, with a ribbon about his neck, was not very bad. This copy procured a piece of good luck for the young artist.

Pere Issacar, a bric-a-brac merchant on the Quay Voltairean—an old-fashioned Jew with a filthy overcoat, the very sight of which made one long to tear it off—approached Maria one day, just as she was about to sketch a rose in the Marquise's powdered wig, and after raising a hat greasy enough to make the soup for a whole regiment, said to her:

"Matemoiselle, vould you make me von dozen vamily bordraits?"

The young girl did not at first understand his abominable language, but at last he made her comprehend.

Every thing is bought nowadays, even rank, provided, of course, that one has a purse sufficiently well filled. Nothing is simpler! In return for a little money you can procure at the Vatican—second corridor on your right, third door at the left—a brand-new title of Roman Count. A heraldic agency—see advertisement—will plant and make grow at your will a genealogical tree, under whose shade you can give a country breakfast to twenty-five people. You buy a castle with port-holes—port-holes are necessary—in a corner of some reactionary province. You call upon the lords of the surrounding castles with a gold fleur-de-lys in your cravat. You pose as an enraged Legitimist and ferocious Clerical. You give dinners and hunting parties, and the game is won. I will wager that your son will marry into a Faubourg St.-Germain family, a family which descends authentically from the Crusaders.

In order to execute this agreeable buffoonery, you must not forget certain accessories—particularly portraits of your ancestors. They should ornament the castle walls where you regale the country nobles. One must use tact in the selection of this family gallery. There must be no exaggeration. Do not look too high. Do not claim as a founder of your race a knight in armor hideously painted, upon wood, with his coat of arms in one corner of the panel. Bear in mind the date of chivalry. Be satisfied with the head of a dynasty whose gray beard hangs over a well-crimped ruff. I saw a very good example of that kind the other day on the Place Royale. A dog was just showing his disrespect for it as I passed. You can obtain an ancestor like this in the outskirts of the city for fifteen francs, if you haggle a little. Or you need not give yourself so much trouble. Apply to a specialist, Pere Issacar, for instance. He will procure magnificent ancestors for you; not dear either! If you will consent to descend to simple magistrates, the price will be insignificant. Chief justices are dirt cheap. Naturally, if you wish to be of the military profession, to have eminent clergy among your antecedents, the price increases. Pere Issacar is the only one who can give you, at a reasonable rate, ermine-draped bishops, or a colonel with a Louis XIV wig, and, if you wish it, a blue ribbon and a breast-plate under his red coat. What produces a good effect in a series of family portraits is a series of pastels. What would you say to a goggle-eyed abbe, or an old lady indecently decolletee, or a captain of dragoons wearing a tigerskin cap (it is ten francs more if he has the cross of St. Louis)? Pere Issacar knows his business, and always has in reserve thirty of these portraits in charming frames of the period, made expressly for him in the Faubourg St.-Antoine, and which have all been buried fifteen days and riddled with shot, in order to have the musty appearance and indispensable worm holes.

You can understand now why the estimable Jew, in passing through the Louvre for his weekly promenade, took an interest in little Maria copying the charming Marquise de Latour. He was just at this time short of powdered marquises, and they are always very much in demand. He begged the young woman to take her copy home and make twelve more of it, varying, only the color of the dress and some particular detail in each portrait. Thus, instead of the pug dog, marquise No. 2 would hold a King Charles spaniel, No. 2 a monkey, No. 3 a bonbon box, No. 4 a fan. The face could remain the same. All marquises looked alike to Pere Issacar; he only exacted that they should all be provided with two black patches, one under the right eye, the other on the left shoulder. This he insisted upon, for the patch, in his eyes, was a symbol of the eighteenth century.

Pere Issacar was a fair man and promised to furnish frames, paper, and pastels, and to pay the young girl fifteen francs for each marquise. What was better yet, he promised, if he was pleased with the first work, to order of the young artist a dozen canonesses of Remiremont and a half-dozen of royal gendarmes.

I wish you could have seen those ladies when Maria went home to tell the good news. Louise had just returned from distributing semiquavers in the city; her eyes and poor Mother Gerard's were filled with tears of joy.

"What, my darling," said the mother, embracing her child, "are you going to trouble yourself about our necessaries of life, too?"

"Do you see this little sister?" said Louise, laughing cordially. "She is going to earn a pile of money as large as she is herself. Do you know that I am jealous—I, with my piano and my displeasing profession? Good-luck to pastel! It is not noisy, it will not annoy the neighbors, and when you are old you can say, 'I never have played for anybody.'"

But Maria did not wish them to joke. They had always treated her like a doll, a spoiled child, who only knew how to curl her hair and tumble her frocks. Well, they should see!

When Amedee arrived on Sunday with his cake, they told him over several times the whole story, with a hundred details, and showed him the two marquises that Maria had already finished, who wore patches as large as wafers.

She appeared that day more attractive and charming than ever to the young man, and it was then that he conceived his first ambition. If he only had enough talent to get out of his obscurity and poverty, and could become a famous writer and easily earn his living! It was not impossible, after all. Oh, with what pleasure he would ask this exquisite child to be his wife! How sweet it would be to know that she was happy with, and proud of, him! But he must not think of it now, they were too poor; and then, would Maria love him?

He often asked himself that question, and with uneasiness. In his own heart he felt that the childish intimacy had become a sincere affection, a real love. He had no reason to hope that the same transformation had taken place in the young girl's heart. She always treated him very affectionately, but rather like a good comrade, and she was no more stirred by his presence now than she was when she had lain in wait with him behind the old green sofa to hunt Father Gerard's battered fur hat.

Amedee had most naturally taken the Gerard family into his confidence regarding his work. After the Sunday dinner they would seat themselves around the table where Mamma Gerard had just served the coffee, and the young man would read to his friends, in a grave, slow voice, the poem he had composed during the week. A painter having the taste and inclination for interior scenes, like the old masters of the Dutch school, would have been stirred by the contemplation of this group of four persons in mourning. The poet, with his manuscript in his right hand and marking the syllables with a rhythmical movement of his left, was seated between the two sisters. But while Louise—a little too thin and faded for her years—fixes her attentive eyes upon the reader and listens with avidity, the pretty Maria is listless and sits with a bored little face, gazing mechanically at the other side of the table. Mother Gerard knits with a serious air and her spectacles perched upon the tip of her nose.

Alas! during these readings Louise was the only one who heaved sighs of emotion; and sometimes even great tear-drops would tremble upon her lashes. She was the only one who could find just the right delicate word with which to congratulate the poet, and show that she had understood and been touched by his verses. At the most Maria would sometimes accord the young poet, still agitated by the declamation of his lines, a careless "It is very pretty!" with a commonplace smile of thanks.

She did not care for poetry, then? Later, if he married her, would she remain indifferent to her husband's intellectual life, insensible even to the glory that he might reap? How sad it was for Amedee to have to ask himself that question!

Soon Maria inspired a new fear within him. Maurice and his mother had been already three months in Italy, and excepting two letters that he had received from Milan, at the beginning of his journey, in the first flush of his enthusiasm, Amedee had had no news from his friend. He excused this negligence on the part of the lazy Maurice, who had smilingly told him, on the eve of departure, not to count upon hearing from him regularly. At each visit that Amedee paid the Gerards, Maria always asked him:

"Have you received any news from your friend Maurice?"

At first he had paid no attention to this, but her persistency at length astonished him, planting a little germ of suspicion and alarm in his heart. Maurice Roger had only paid the Gerards a few visits during the father's lifetime, and accompanied on each occasion by Amedee. He had always observed the most respectful manner toward Maria, and they had perhaps exchanged twenty words. Why should Maria preserve such a particular remembrance of a person so nearly a stranger to her? Was it possible that he had made a deep impression, perhaps even inspired a sentiment of love? Did she conceal in the depths of her heart, when she thought of him, a tender hope? Was she watching for him? Did she wish him to return?

When these fears crossed Amedee's mind, he felt a choking sensation, and his heart was troubled. Happy Maurice, who had only to be seen to please! But immediately, with a blush of shame, the generous poet chased away this jealous fancy. But every Sunday, when Maria, lowering her eyes, and with a slightly embarrassed voice, repeated her question, "Have you received any news from Monsieur Maurice?" Amedee felt a cruelly discouraged feeling, and thought, with deep sadness:

"She never will love me!"

To conquer this new grief, he plunged still more deeply into work; but he did not find his former animation and energy. After the drizzling rain of the last days of March, the spring arrived. Now, when Amedee awoke, it was broad daylight at six o'clock in the morning. Opening his mansard window, he admired, above the tops of the roofs, the large, ruddy sun rising in the soft gray sky, and from the convent gardens beneath came a fresh odor of grass and damp earth. Under the shade of the arched lindens which led to the shrine of a plaster Virgin, a first and almost imperceptible rustle, a presentiment of verdure, so to speak, ran through the branches, and the three almond trees in the kitchen-garden put forth their delicate flowers. The young poet was invaded by a sweet and overwhelming languor, and Maria's face, which was commonly before his inner vision upon awakening, became confused and passed from his mind. He seated himself for a moment before a table and reread the last lines of a page that he had begun; but he was immediately overcome by physical lassitude, and abandoned himself to thought, saying to himself that he was twenty years old, and that it would be very good, after all, to enjoy life.

CHAPTER X

A BUDDING POET

It is the first of May, and the lilacs in the Luxembourg Gardens are in blossom. It has just struck four o'clock. The bright sun and the pure sky have rendered more odious than ever the captivity of the office to Amedee, and he departs before the end of the sitting for a stroll in the Medicis garden around the pond, where, for the amusement of the children in that quarter, a little breeze from the northeast is pushing on a miniature flotilla. Suddenly he hears himself called by a voice which bursts out like a brass band at a country fair.

"Good-day, Violette."

It is Jocquelet, the future comedian, with his turned-up nose, which cuts the air like the prow of a first-class ironclad, superb, triumphant, dressed like a Brazilian, shaved to the quick, the dearest hope of Regnier's class at the Conservatoire-Jocquelet, who has made an enormous success in an act from the "Precieuses," at the last quarter's examination—he says so himself, without any useless modesty—Jocquelet, who will certainly have the first comedy prize at the next examination, and will make his debut with out delay at the Comedie Francaise! All this he announces in one breath, like a speech learned by heart, with his terrible voice, like a quack selling shaving-paste from a gilded carriage. In two minutes that favorite word of theatrical people had been repeated thirty times, punctuating the phrases: "I! I! I! I!"

Amedee is only half pleased at the meeting. Jocquelet was always a little too noisy to please him. After all, he was an old comrade, and out of politeness the poet congratulated him upon his success.

Jocquelet questioned him. What was Amedee doing? What had become of him? Where was his literary work? All this was asked with such cordiality and warmth of manner that one would have thought that Jocquelet was interested in Amedee, and had a strong friendship for him. Nothing of the, sort. Jocquelet was interested in only one person in this world, and that person was named Jocquelet. One is either an actor or he is not. This personage was always one wherever he was—in an omnibus, while putting on his suspenders, even with the one he loved. When he said to a newcomer, "How do you do?" he put so much feeling into this very original question, that the one questioned asked himself whether he really had not just recovered from a long and dangerous illness. Now, at this time Jocquelet found himself in the presence of an unknown and poor young poet. What role ought such an eminent person as himself to play in such circumstances? To show affection for the young man, calm his timidity, and patronize him without too much haughtiness; that was the position to take, and Jocquelet acted it.

Amedee was an artless dupe, and, touched by the interest shown him, he frankly replied:

"Well, my dear friend, I have worked hard this winter. I am not dissatisfied. I think that I have made some progress; but if you knew how hard and difficult it is!"

He was about to confide to Jocquelet the doubts and sufferings of a sincere artist, but Jocquelet, as we have said, thought only of himself, and brusquely interrupted the young poet:

"You do not happen to have a poem with you—something short, a hundred or a hundred and fifty lines—a poem intended for effect, that one could recite?"

Amedee had copied out that very day, at the office, a war story, a heroic episode of Sebastopol that he had heard Colonel Lantz relate not long since at Madame Roger's, and had put into verse with a good French sentiment and quite the military spirit, verse which savored of powder, and went off like reports of musketry. He took the sheets out of his pocket, and, leading the comedian into a solitary by-path of sycamores which skirted the Luxembourg orangery, he read his poem to him in a low voice. Jocquelet, who did not lack a certain literary instinct, was very enthusiastic, for he foresaw a success for himself, and said to the poet:

"You read those verses just like a poet, that is, very badly. But no matter, this battle is very effective, and I see what I could do with it-with my voice. But what do you mean?" added he, planting himself in front of his friend. "Do you write verses like these and nobody knows anything about them? It is absurd. Do you wish, then, to imitate Chatterton? That is an old game, entirely used up! You must push yourself, show yourself. I will take charge of that myself! Your evening is free, is it not? Very well, come with me; before six o'clock I shall have told your name to twenty trumpeters, who will make all Paris resound with the news that there is a poet in the Faubourg Saint-Jacques. I will wager, you savage, that you never have put your foot into the Cafe de Seville. Why, my dear fellow, it is our first manufactory of fame! Here is the Odeon omnibus, get on! We shall be at the Boulevard Montmartre in twenty minutes, and I shall baptize you there, as a great man, with a glass of absinthe."

Dazzled and carried away, Amedee humored him and climbed upon the outside of the omnibus with his comrade. The vehicle hurried them quickly along toward the quay, crossed the Seine, the Carrousel, and passed before the Theatre-Francais, at which Jocquelet, thinking of his approaching debut, shook his fist, exclaiming, "Now I am ready for you!" Here the young men were planted upon the asphalt boulevard, in front of the Cafe de Seville.

Do not go to-day to see this old incubator, in which so many political and literary celebrities have been hatched; for you will only find a cafe, just like any other, with its groups of ugly little Jews who discuss the coming races, and here and there a poor creature, painted like a Jezebel, dying of chagrin over her pot of beer.

At the decline of the Second Empire—it was May 1, 1866, that Amedee Violette entered there for the first time—the Cafe de, Seville passed for, and with reason too, one of the most remarkable places in Paris. For this glorious establishment had furnished by itself, or nearly so, the eminent staff of our third

Republic! Be honest, Monsieur le Prefet, you who presided at the opening of the agricultural meeting in our province, and who played the peacock in your dress-coat, embroidered in silver, before an imposing line of horned creatures; be honest and admit, that, at the time when you opposed the official candidates in your democratic journal, you had your pipe in the rack of the Cafe de Seville, with your name in white enamel upon the blackened bowl! Remember, Monsieur le Depute, you who voted against all the exemption cases of the military law, remember who, in this very place, at your daily game of dominoes for sixty points, more than a hundred times ranted against the permanent army—you, accustomed to the uproar of assemblies and the noise of the tavern—contributed to the parliamentary victories by crying, "Six all! count that!" And you too, Monsieur le Ministre, to whom an office-boy, dating from the tyrants, still says, "Your excellency," without offending you; you also have been a constant frequenter of the Cafe de Seville, and such a faithful customer that the cashier calls you by your Christian name. And do you recall, Monsieur the future president of the Council, that you did not acquit yourself very well when the sedentary dame, who never has been seen to rise from her stool, and who, as a joker pretended, was afflicted with two wooden legs, called you by a little sign to the desk, and said to you, not without a shade of severity in her tone: "Monsieur Eugene, we must be thinking of this little bill."

Notwithstanding his title of poet, Amedee had not the gift of prophecy. While seeing all these negligently dressed men seated outside at the Cafe de Seville's tables, taking appetizers, the young man never suspected that he had before him the greater part of the legislators destined to assure, some years later, France's happiness. Otherwise he would have respectfully taken note of each drinker and the color of his drink, since at a later period this would have been very useful to him as a mnemonical method for the understanding of our parliamentary combinations, which are a little complicated, we must admit. For example, would it not have been handy and agreeable to note down that the recent law on sugars had been voted by the solid majority of absinthe and bitters, or to know that the Cabinet's fall, day before yesterday, might be attributed simply to the disloyal and perfidious abandonment of the bitter mints or blackcurrant wine?

Jocquelet, who professed the most advanced opinions in politics, distributed several riotous and patronizing handshakes among these future statesmen as he entered the establishment, followed by Amedee.

Here, there were still more of politics, and also poets and literary men. They lived a sort of hurly-burly life, on good terms, but one could not get them confounded, for the politicians were all beard, the litterateurs, all hair.

Jocquelet directed his steps without hesitation toward the magnificent red head of the whimsical poet, Paul Sillery, a handsome young fellow with a wide-awake face, who was nonchalantly stretched upon the red velvet cushion of the window-seat, before a table, around which were three other heads of thick hair worthy of our early kings.

"My dear Paul," said Jocquelet, in his most thrilling voice, handing Sillery Amedee's manuscript, "here are some verses that I think are superb, and I am going to recite them as soon as I can, at some entertainment or benefit. Read them and give us your opinion of them. I present their author to you, Monsieur Amedee Violette. Amedee, I present you to Monsieur Paul Sillery."

All the heads of hair, framing young and amiable faces, turned curiously toward the newcomer, whom Paul Sillery courteously invited to be seated, with the established formula, "What will you take?" Then he began to read the lines that the comedian had given him.

Amedee, seated on the edge of his chair, was distracted with timidity, for Paul Sillery already enjoyed a certain reputation as a rising poet, and had established a small literary sheet called La Guepe, which published upon its first page caricatures of celebrated men with large heads and little bodies, and Amedee had read in it some of Paul's poems, full of impertinence and charm. An author whose work had been published! The editor of a journal! The idea was stunning to poor innocent Violette, who was not aware then that La Guepe could not claim forty subscribers. He considered Sillery something wonderful, and waited with a beating heart for the verdict of so formidable a judge. At the end of a few moments Sillery said, without raising his eyes from the manuscript:

"Here are some fine verses!"

A flood of delight filled the heart of the poet from the Faubourg St.-Jacques.

As soon as he had finished his reading, Paul arose from his seat, and, extending both hands over the carafes and glasses to Amedee, said, enthusiastically:

"Let me shake hands with you! Your description of the battle-scene is astonishing! It is admirable! It is as clear and precise as Merimee, and it has all the color and imagination that he lacks to make him a poet. It is something absolutely new. My dear Monsieur Violette, I congratulate you with all my heart! I can not ask you for this beautiful poem for La Guepe that Jocquelet is so fortunate as to have to recite, and of which I hope he will make a success. But I beg of you, as a great favor, to let me have some verses for my paper; they will be, I am sure, as good as these, if not better. To be sure, I forgot to tell you that we shall not be able to pay you for the copy, as La Guepe does not prosper; I will even admit that it only stands on one leg. In order to make it appear for a few months longer, I have recently been obliged to go to a money-lender, who has left me, instead of the classical stuffed crocodile, a trained horse which he had just taken from an insolvent circus. I mounted the noble animal to go to the Bois, but at the Place de la Concorde he began to waltz around it, and I was obliged to get rid of this dancing quadruped at a considerable loss. So your contribution to La Guepe would have to be gratuitous, like those of all the rest. You will give me the credit of having saluted you first of all, my dear Violette, by the rare and glorious title of true poet. You will let me reserve the pleasure of intoxicating you with the odor that a printer's first proofs give, will you not? Is it agreed?"

Yes, it was agreed! That is to say, Amedee, touched to the depths of his heart by so much good grace and fraternal cordiality, was so troubled in trying to find words to express his gratitude, that he made a terrible botch of it.

"Do not thank me," said Paul Sillery, with his pleasant but rather sceptical smile, "and do not think me better than I am. If all your verses are as strong as these that I have just read, you will soon publish a volume that will make a sensation, and—who knows?—perhaps will inspire me first of all with an ugly attack of jealousy. Poets are no better than other people; they are like the majority of Adam's sons, vain and envious, only they still keep the ability to admire, and the gift of enthusiasm, and that proves their superiority and is to their credit. I am delighted to have found a mare's nest to-day, an original and sincere poet, and with your permission we will celebrate this happy meeting. The price of the waltzing horse having hardly sufficed to pay off the debt to the publisher of La Guepe, I am not in funds this evening; but I have credit at Pere Lebuffle's, and I invite you all to dinner at his pot-house; after which we will go to my rooms, where I expect a few friends, and there you will read us your verses, Violette; we will all read some of them, and have a fine orgy of rich rhymes."

This proposition was received with favor by the three young men with the long hair, a la Clodion and Chilperic. As for Violette, he would have followed Paul Sillery at that moment, had it been into the infernal regions.

Jocquelet could not go with them, he had promised his evening to a lady, he said, and he gave this excuse with such a conceited smile that all were convinced he was going to crown himself with the most flattering of laurels at the mansion of some princess of the royal blood. In reality, he was going to see one of his Conservatoire friends, a large, lanky dowdy, as swarthy as a mole and full of pretensions, who was destined for the tragic line of character, and inflicted upon her lover Athalie's dream, Camille's imprecations, and Phedre's monologue.

After paying for the refreshments, Sillery gave his arm to Amedee, and, followed by the three Merovingians, they left the cafe. Forcing a way through the crowd which obstructed the sidewalk of the Faubourg Montmartre he conducted his guests to Pere Lebuffle's table d'hote, which was situated on the third floor of a dingy old house in the Rue Lamartine, where a sickening odor of burnt meat greeted them as soon as they reached the top of the stairs. They found there, seated before a tablecloth remarkable for the number of its wine-stains, two or three wild-looking heads of hair, and four or five shaggy beards, to whom Pere Lebuffle was serving soup, aided by a tired-looking servant. The name under which Sillery had designated the proprietor of the table d'hote might have been a nickname, for this stout person in his shirt-sleeves recommended himself to one's attentions by his bovine face and his gloomy, wandering eyes. To Amedee's amazement, Pere Lebuffle called the greater part of his clients "thou," and as soon as the newcomers were seated at table, Amedee asked Sillery, in a low voice, the cause of this familiarity.

"It is caused by the hard times, my dear Violette," responded the editor of 'La Guepe' as he unfolded his napkin. "There is no longer a 'Maecenas' or

'Lawrence the Magnificent.' The last patron of literature and art is Pere Lebufle. This wretched cook, who has perhaps never read a book or seen a picture, has a fancy for painters and poets, and allows them to cultivate that plant, Debt, which, contrary to other vegetables, grows all the more, the less it is watered with instalments. We must pardon the good man," said he, lowering his voice, "his little sin—a sort of vanity. He wishes to be treated like a comrade and friend by the artists. Those who have several accounts brought forward upon his ledger, arrive at the point of calling him 'thou,' and I, alas! am of that number. Thanks to that, I am going to make you drink something a little less purgative than the so-called wine which is turning blue in that carafe, and of which I advise you to be suspicious. I say, Lebuffle, my friend here, Monsieur Amedee Violette, will be, sooner or later, a celebrated poet. Treat him accordingly, my good fellow, and go and get us a bottle of Moulins-Vent."

The conversation meanwhile became general between the bearded and long-haired men. Is it necessary to say that they were all animated, both politicians and 'litterateurs', with the most revolutionary sentiments? At the very beginning, with the sardines, which evidently had been pickled in lamp-oil, a terribly hairy man, the darkest of them all, with a beard that grew up into its owner's eyes and then sprung out again in tufts from his nose and ears, presented some elegiac regrets to the memory of Jean-Paul Marat, and declared that at the next revolution it would be necessary to realize the programme of that delightful friend of the people, and make one hundred thousand heads fall.

"By thunder, Flambard, you have a heavy hand!" exclaimed one of the least important of beards, one of those that degenerate into side-whiskers as they become conservative. "One hundred thousand heads!"

"It is the minimum," replied the sanguinary beard.

Now, it had just been revealed to Amedee that under this ferocious beard was concealed a photographer, well known for his failures, and the young man could not help thinking that if the one hundred thousand heads in question had posed before the said Flambard's camera, he would not show such impatience to see them fall under the guillotine.

The conversation of the men with the luxuriant hair was none the less anarchical when the roast appeared, which sprung from the legendary animal called 'vache enragee'. The possessor of the longest and thickest of all the shock heads, which spread over the shoulders of a young story writer—between us, be it said, he made a mistake in not combing it oftener—imparted to his brothers the subject for his new novel, which should have made the hair of the others bristle with terror; for the principal episode in this agreeable fiction was the desecration of a dead body in a cemetery by moonlight. There was a sort of hesitation in the audience, a slight movement of recoil, and Sillery, with a dash of raillery in his glance, asked the novelist:

"Why the devil do you write such a story?"

The novelist replied, in a thundering tone:

"To astonish the bourgeoisie!"

And nobody made the slightest objection.

To "astonish the bourgeoisie" was the dearest hope and most ardent wish of these young men, and this desire betrayed itself in their slightest word; and doubtless Amedee thought it legitimate and even worthy of praise. However, he did not believe—must we admit his lack of confidence?—that so many glorious efforts were ever crowned with success. He went so far as to ask himself whether the character and cleverness of these bourgeoisie would not lead them to ignore not only the works, but even the existence, of the authors who sought to "astonish" them; and he thought, not without sadness, that when La Guepe should have published this young novelist's ghostly composition, the unconquerable bourgeoisie would know nothing about it, and would continue to devote itself to its favorite customs, such as tapping the barometer to know whether there was a change, or to heave a deep sigh after guzzling its soup, saying, "I feel better!" without being the least astonished in the world.

In spite of these mental reservations, which Amedee reproached himself with, being himself an impure and contemptible Philistine, the poet was delighted with his new friends and the unknown world opening before him. In this Bohemian corner, where one got intoxicated with wild excesses and paradoxes, recklessness and gayety reigned. The sovereign charm of youth was there, and Amedee, who had until now lived in a dark hiding-place, blossomed out in this warm atmosphere.

After a horrible dessert of cheese and prunes, Pere Lebuffle's guests dispersed. Sillery escorted Amedee and the three Merovingians to the little, sparsely furnished first floor in the Rue Pigalle, where he lived; and half a dozen other lyric poets, who might have furnished some magnificent trophies for an Apache warrior's scalping-knife, soon came to reenforce the club which met there every Wednesday evening.

Seats were wanting at the beginning, but Sillery drew from a closet an old black trunk which would hold two, and contented himself, as master of the house, with sitting from time to time, with legs dangling, upon the marble mantel. The company thus found themselves very comfortable; still more so when an old woman with a dirty cap had placed upon the table, in the middle of the room, six bottles of beer, some odd glasses, and a large flowered plate upon which was a package of cut tobacco with cigarette paper. They began to recite their verses in a cloud of smoke. Each recited his own, called upon by Sillery; each would rise without being urged, place his chair in front of him, and leaning one hand upon its back, would recite his poem or elegy. Certainly some of them were wanting in genius, some were even ludicrous. Among the number was a little fellow with a cadaverous face, about as large as two farthings' worth of butter, who declared, in a long speech with flat rhymes, that an Asiatic harem was not capable of quenching his ardent love of pleasure. A fat-faced fellow with a good, healthy, country complexion, announced, in a long story, his formal intention of dying of a decline, on account of the treason of a courtesan with a face as cold as marble; while, if the facts were known, this peaceable boy lived with an artless child of the people, brightening her lot by reducing her to a state of slavery; she blacked his boots for him every morning before he left the house.

In spite of these ridiculous things, there were present some genuine poets who knew their business and had real talent. These filled Amedee with respect and fear, and when Sillery called his name, he arose with a dry mouth and heavy heart.

"It is your turn now, you newcomer! Recite us your 'Before Sebastopol.'"

And so, thoroughbred that he was, Amedee overcame his emotion and recited, in a thrilling voice, his military rhymes, that rang out like the report of a veteran's gun.

The last stanza, was greeted with loud applause, and all the auditors arose and surrounded Amedee to offer him their congratulations.

"Why, it is superb!"

"Entirely new!"

"It will make an enormous success!"

"It is just what is needed to arouse the public!"

"Recite us something else!—something else!"

Reassured and encouraged, master of himself, he recited a popular scene in which he had freely poured out his love for the poor people. He next recited some of his Parisian suburban scenes, and then a series of sonnets, entitled "Love's Hopes," inspired by his dear Maria; and he astonished all these poets by the versatility and variety of his inspirations.

At each new poem bravos were thundered out, and the young man's heart expanded with joy under this warm sunshine of success. His audience vied with each other to approach Amedee first, and to shake his hand. Alas! some of those who were there would, later, annoy him by their low envy and treason; but now, in the generous frankness of their youth, they welcomed him as a master.

What an intoxicating evening! Amedee reached his home about two o'clock in the morning, his hands burning with the last grasps, his brain and heart intoxicated with the strong wine of praise. He walked with long and joyful strides through the fairy scene of a beautiful moonlight, in the fresh morning wind which made his clothes flutter and caressed his face. He thought he even felt the breath of fame.

A ROMANCE OF YOUTH

By FRANCOIS COPPEE

BOOK 3.

CHAPTER XI

SUCCESS

Success, which usually is as fickle as justice, took long strides and doubled its stations in order to reach Amedee. The Cafe de Seville, and the coterie of long-haired writers, were busying themselves with the rising poet already. His suite of sonnets, published in La Guepe, pleased some of the journalists, who reproduced them in portions in well-distributed journals. Ten days after Amedee's meeting with Jocquelet, the latter recited his poem "Before Sebastopol" at a magnificent entertainment given at the Gaite for the benefit of an illustrious actor who had become blind and reduced to poverty.

This "dramatic solemnity," to use the language of the advertisement, began by being terribly tiresome. There was an audience present who were accustomed to grand Parisian soirees, a blase and satiated public, who, upon this warm evening in the suffocating theatre, were more fatigued and satiated than ever. The sleepy journalists collapsed in their chairs, and in the back part of the stage-boxes, ladies' faces, almost green under paint, showed the excessive lassitude of a long winter of pleasure. The Parisians had all come there from custom, without having the slightest desire to do so, just as they always came, like galley-slaves condemned to "first nights." They were so lifeless that they did not even feel the slightest horror at seeing one another grow old. This chloroformed audience was afflicted with a long and too heavy programme, as is the custom in performances of this kind. They played fragments of the best known pieces, and sang songs from operas long since fallen into disuse even on street organs. This public saw the same comedians march out; the most famous are the most monotonous; the comical ones abused their privileges; the lover spoke distractedly through his nose; the great coquette—the actress par excellence, the last of the Celimenes —discharged her part in such a sluggish way that when she began an adverb ending in "ment," one would have almost had time to go out and smoke a cigarette or drink a glass of beer before she reached the end of the said adverb.

But at the most lethargic moment of this drowsy soirees, after the comedians from the Francais had played in a stately manner one act from a tragedy, Jocquelet appeared. Jocquelet, still a pupil at the Conservatoire, showed himself to the public for the first time and by an exceptional grace—Jocquelet, absolutely unknown, too short in his evening clothes, in spite of the two packs of cards that he had put in his boots. He appeared, full of audacity, riding his high horse, raising his flat-nosed, bull-dog face toward the "gallery gods," and, in his voice capable of making Jericho's wall fall or raising Jehoshaphat's dead, he dashed off in one effort, but with intelligence and heroic feeling, his comrade's poem.

The effect was prodigious. This bold, common, but powerful actor, and these picturesque and modern verses were something entirely new to this public satiated with old trash. What a happy surprise! Two novelties at once! To think of discovering an unheard-of poet and an unknown comedian! To nibble at these two green fruits! Everybody shook off his torpor; the anaesthetized journalists aroused themselves; the colorless and sleepy ladies plucked up a little animation; and when Jocquelet had made the last rhyme resound like a grand flourish of trumpets, all applauded enough to split their gloves.

In one of the theatre lobbies, behind a bill-board pasted over with old placards, Amedee Violette heard with delight the sound of the applause which seemed like a shower of hailstones. He dared not think of it! Was it really his poem that produced so much excitement, which had thawed this cold public? Soon he did not doubt it, for Jocquelet, who had just been recalled three times, threw himself into the poet's arms and glued his perspiring, painted face to his.

"Well, my little one, I have done it!" he exclaimed, bursting with gratification and vanity. "You heard how I caught them!"

Immediately twenty, thirty, a hundred spectators appeared, most of them very correct in white cravats, but all eager and with beaming countenances, asking to see the author and the interpreter, and to be presented to them, that they might congratulate them with an enthusiastic word and a shake of the hand. Yes! it was a success, an instantaneous one. It was certainly that rare tropical flower of the Parisian greenhouse which blossoms out so seldom, but so magnificently.

One large, very common-looking man, wearing superb diamond shirt-buttons, came in his turn to shake Amedee's hand, and in a hoarse, husky voice which would have been excellent to propose tickets "cheaper than at the office!" he asked for the manuscript of the poem that had just been recited.

"It is so that I may put you upon the first page of my tomorrow's edition, young man, and I publish eighty thousand. Victor Gaillard, editor of 'Le Tapage'. Does that please you?"

He took the manuscript without listening to the thanks of the poet, who trembled with joy at the thought that his work had caught the fancy of this Barnum of the press, the foremost advertiser in France and Europe, and that his verses would meet the eyes of two hundred thousand readers.

Yes, it was certainly a success, and he experienced the first bitterness of it as soon as he arrived the next morning at the Cafe de Seville, where he now went every two or three days at the hour for absinthe. His verses had appeared in that morning's Tapage, printed in large type and headed by a few lines of praise written by Victor Gaillard, a la Barnum. As soon as Amedee entered the cafe he saw that he was the object of general attention, and the lyric gentlemen greeted him with acclamations and bravos; but at certain expressions of countenance, constrained looks, and bitter smiles, the impressionable young man felt with a sudden sadness that they already envied him.

"I warned you of it," said Paul Sillery to him, as he led him into a corner of the cafe. "Our good friends are not pleased, and that is very natural. The greater part of these rhymers are 'cheap jewellers,' and they are jealous of a master workman. Above all things, pretend not to notice it; they will never forgive you for guessing their bad sentiments. And then you must be indulgent to them. You have your beautiful lieutenant's epaulettes, Violette, do not be too hard upon these poor privates. They also are fighting under the poetic flag, and ours is a poverty-stricken regiment. Now you must profit by your good luck. Here you are, celebrated in forty-eight hours. Do you see, even the political people look at you with curiosity, although a poet in the estimation of these austere persons is an inferior and useless being. It is all they will do to accept Victor Hugo, and only on account of his 'Chatiments.' You are the lion of the day. Lose no time. I met just now upon the boulevard Massif, the publisher. He had read 'Le Tapage' and expects you. Carry him all your poems to-morrow; there will be enough to make a volume. Massif will publish it at his own expense, and you will appear before the public in one month. You never will inveigle a second time that big booby of a Gaillard, who took a mere passing fancy for you. But no matter! I know your book, and it will be a success. You are launched. Forward, march! Truly, I am better than I thought, for your success gives me pleasure."

This amiable comrade's words easily dissipated the painful feelings that Amedee had just experienced. However, it was one of those exalted moments when one will not admit that evil exists. He spent some time with the poets, forcing himself to be more gracious and friendly than ever, and left them persuaded—the unsuspecting child!—that he had disarmed them by his modesty; and very impatient to share his joy with his friends, the Gerards, he quickly walked the length of Montmartre and reached them just at their dinner hour.

They did not expect him, and only had for their dinner the remains of the boiled beef of the night before, with some cucumbers. Amedee carried his cake, as usual, and, what was better still, two sauces that always make the poorest meal palatable—hope and happiness.

They had already read the journals and knew that the poem had been applauded at the Gaite, and that it had at once been printed on the first page of the journal; and they were all so pleased, so glad, that they kissed Amedee on both cheeks. Mamma Gerard remembered that she had a few bottles—five or six—of old chambertin in the cellar, and you could not have prevented the excellent woman from taking her key and taper at once, and going for those old bottles covered with cobwebs and dust, that they might drink to the health of the triumphant one. As to Louise, she was radiant, for in several houses where she gave lessons she had heard them talk of the fine and admirable verses published in Le Tapage, and she was very proud to think that the author was a friend of hers. What completed Amedee's pleasure was that for the first time Maria seemed to be interested in his poem, and said several times to him, with such a pretty, vain little air:

"Do you know, your battle is very nice. Amedee, you are going to become a great poet, a celebrated man! What a superb future you have before you!"

Ah! what exquisitely sweet hopes he carried away that evening to his room in the Faubourg St.-Jacques! They gave him beautiful dreams, and pervaded his thoughts the next morning when the concierge brought him two letters.

Still more happiness! The first letter contained two notes of a hundred francs each, with Victor Gaillard's card, who congratulated Amedee anew and asked him to write something for his journal in the way of prose; a story, or anything he liked. The young poet gave a cry of joyful surprise when he recognized the handwriting of Maurice Roger upon the other envelope.

"I have just returned to Paris, my dear Amedee," wrote the traveller, "and your success was my first greeting. I must embrace you quickly and tell you how happy I am. Come to see me at four o'clock in my den in the Rue Monsieur-le-Prince. We will dine and pass the evening together."

Ah! how the poet loved life that morning, how good and sweet it seemed to him! Clothed in his best, he gayly descended the Rue St.-Jacques, where boxes of asparagus and strawberries perfumed the fruit-stalls, and went to the Boulevard St. Michel, where he purchased an elegant gray felt hat and a new cravat. Then he went to the Cafe Voltaire, where he lunched. He changed his second hundred-franc bill, so that he might feel, with the pleasure of a child, the beautiful louis d'or which he owed to his work and its success. At the office the head clerk—a good fellow, who sang well at dinners—complimented Amedee upon his poem. The young man had only made his appearance to ask for leave that afternoon, so as to take his manuscript to the publisher.

Once more in the street in the bright May sun, after the fashion of nabobs, he took an open carriage and was carried to Massif, in the Passage des Princes. The editor of the Jeunes was seated in his office, which was decorated with etchings and beautiful bindings. He is well known by his magnificent black beard and his large bald head, upon which a wicked jester once advised him to paste his advertisements; he publishes the works of audacious authors and sensational books, and had the honor of sharing with Charles Bazile, the poet, an imprisonment at St.-Pelagie. He received this thin-faced rhymer coldly. Amedee introduced himself, and at once there was a broad smile, a handshake, and a connoisseur's greedy sniffling. Then Massif opened the manuscript.

"Let us see! Ah, yes, with margins and false titles we can make out two hundred and fifty pages."

The business was settled quickly. A sheet of stamped paper—an agreement! Massif will pay all the expenses of the first edition of one thousand, and if there is another edition—and of course there will be!—he will give him ten cents a copy. Amedee signs without reading. All that he asks is that the volume should be published without delay.

"Rest easy, my dear poet! You will receive the first proofs in three days, and in one month it will appear."

Was it possible? Was Amedee not dreaming? He, poor Violette's son, the little office clerk—his book would be published, and in a month! Readers and unknown friends will be moved by his agitation, will suffer in his suspense; young people will love him and find an echo of their sentiments in his verses; women will dreamily repeat—with one finger in his book—some favorite verse that touches their hearts! Ah! he must have a confidant in his joy, he must tell some true friend.

"Driver, take me to the Rue Monsieur-le-Prince."

He mounted, four steps at a time, the stairs leading to Maurice's room. The key is in the door. He enters and finds the traveller there, standing in the midst of the disorder of open trunks.

"Maurice!"

"Amedee!"

What an embrace! How long they stood hand in hand, looking at each other with happy smiles!

Maurice is more attractive and gracious than ever. His beauty is more manly, and his golden moustache glistens against his sun-browned skin. What a fine fellow! How he rejoiced at his friend's first success!

"I am certain that your book will turn everybody's head. I always told you that you were a genuine poet. We shall see!"

As to himself, he was happy too. His mother had let him off from studying law and allowed him to follow his vocation. He was going to have a studio and paint. It had all been decided in Italy, where Madame Roger had witnessed her son's enthusiasm over the great masters. Ah, Italy! Italy! and he began to tell of his trip, show knickknacks and souvenirs of all kinds that littered the room. He turned in his hands, that he might show all its outlines, a little terra-cotta reduction of the Antinous in the Museum of Naples. He opened a box, full to bursting, of large photographs, and passed them to his friend with exclamations of retrospective admiration.

"Look! the Coliseum! the ruins of Paestum—and this antique from the Vatican! Is it not beautiful?"

While looking at the pictures he recalled the things that he had seen and the impressions he had experienced. There was a band of collegians in little capes and short trousers taking their walk; they wore buckled shoes, like the abbes of olden times, and nothing could be more droll than to see these childish priests play leapfrog. There, upon the Riva dei Schiavoni, he had followed a Venetian. "Shabbily dressed, and fancy, my friend, bare-headed, in a yellow shawl with ragged green fringe! No, I do not know whether she was pretty, but she possessed in her person all the attractions of Giorgione's goddesses and Titian's courtesans combined!"

Maurice is still the same wicked fellow. But, bah! it suits him; he even boasts of it with such a joyous ardor and such a youthful dash, that it is only one charm the more in him. The clock struck seven, and they went to dine. They started off through the Latin Quarter. Maurice gave his arm to Amedee and told him of his adventures on the other side of the Alps. Maurice, once started on this subject, could not stop, and while the dinner was being served the traveller continued to describe his escapades. This kind of conversation was dangerous for Amedee;

for it must not be forgotten that for some time the young poet's innocence had weighed upon him, and this evening he had some pieces of gold in his pocket that rang a chime of pleasure. While Maurice, with his elbow upon the table, told him his tales of love, Amedee gazed out upon the sidewalk at the women who passed by in fresh toilettes, in the gaslight which illuminated the green foliage, giving a little nod of the head to those whom they knew. There was voluptuousness in the very air, and it was Amedee who arose from the table and recalled to Maurice that it was Thursday, and that there was a fete that night at Bullier's; and he also was the one to add, with a deliberate air:

"Shall we take a turn there?"

"Willingly," replied his gay friend. "Ah, ha! we are then beginning to enjoy ourselves a little, Monsieur Violette! Go to Bullier's? so be it. I am not sorry to assure myself whether or not I still love the Parisians."

They started off, smoking their cigarettes. Upon the highway, going in the same direction as themselves, were victorias carrying women in spring costumes and wearing bonnets decked with flowers. From time to time the friends were elbowed by students shouting popular refrains and walking in Indian-file.

Here is Bullier's! They step into the blazing entrance, and go thence to the stairway which leads to the celebrated public ballroom. They are stifled by the odor of dust, escaping gas, and human flesh. Alas! there are in every village in France doctors in hansom cabs, country lawyers, and any quantity of justices of the peace, who, I can assure you, regret this stench as they take the fresh air in the open country under the starry heavens, breathing the exquisite perfume of new-mown hay; for it is mingled with the little poetry that they have had in their lives, with their student's love-affairs, and their youth.

All the same, this Bullier's is a low place, a caricature of the Alhambra in pasteboard. Three or four thousand moving heads in a cloud of tobacco-smoke, and an exasperating orchestra playing a quadrille in which dancers twist and turn, tossing their legs with calm faces and audacious gestures.

"What a mob!" said Amedee, already a trifle disgusted. "Let us go into the garden."

They were blinded by the gas there; the thickets looked so much like old scenery that one almost expected to see the yellow breastplates of comic-opera dragoons; and the jet of water recalled one of those little spurts of a shooting-gallery upon which an empty egg-shell dances. But they could breathe there a little.

"Boy! two sodas," said Maurice, striking the table with his cane; and the two friends sat down near the edge of a walk where the crowd passed and repassed. They had been there about ten minutes when two women stopped before them.

"Good-day, Maurice," said the taller, a brunette with rich coloring, the genuine type of a tavern girl.

"What, Margot!" exclaimed the young man. "Will you take something? Sit down a moment, and your friend too. Do you know, your friend is charming? What is her name?"

"Rosine," replied the stranger, modestly, for she was only about eighteen, and, in spite of the blond frizzles over her eyes, she was not yet bold, poor child! She was making her debut, it was easy to see.

"Well, Mademoiselle Rosine, come here, that I may see you," continued Maurice, seating the young girl beside him with a caressing gesture. "You, Margot, I authorize to be unfaithful to me once more in favor of my friend Amedee. He is suffering with lovesickness, and has a heart to let. Although he is a poet, I think he happens to have in his pocket enough to pay for a supper."

Everywhere and always the same, the egotistical and amiable Maurice takes the lion's share, and Amedee, listening only with one ear to the large Margot, who is already begging him to make an acrostic for her, thinks Rosine is charming, while Maurice says a thousand foolish things to her. In spite of himself, the poet looks upon Maurice as his superior, and thinks it perfectly natural that he should claim the prettier of the two women. No matter! Amedee wanted to enjoy himself too. This Margot, who had just taken off her gloves to drink her wine, had large, red hands, and seemed as silly as a goose, but all the same she was a beautiful creature, and the poet began to talk to her, while she laughed and looked at him with a wanton's eyes. Meanwhile the orchestra burst into a polka, and Maurice, in raising his voice to speak to his friend, called him several times Amedee, and once only by his family name, Violette. Suddenly little Rosine started up and looked at the poet, saying with astonishment:

"What! Is your name Amedee Violette?"

"Certainly."

"Then you are the boy with whom I played so much when I was a child."

"With me?"

"Yes! Do you not remember Rosine, little Rosine Combarieu, at Madame Gerard's, the engraver's wife, in the Rue Notre-Dame-des-Champs? We played games with his little girls. How odd it is, the way one meets old friends!"

What is it that Amedee feels? His entire childhood rises before him. The bitterness of the thought that he had known this poor girl in her innocence and youth, and the Gerards' name spoken in such a place, filled the young man's heart with a singular sadness. He could only say to Rosine, in a voice that trembled a little with pity:

"You! Is it you?"

Then she became red and very embarrassed, lowering her eyes.

Maurice had tact; he noticed that Rosine and Amedee were agitated, and, feeling that he was de trop, he arose suddenly and said:

"Now then, Margot. Come on! these children want to talk over their childhood, I think. Give up your acrostic, my child. Take my arm, and come and have a turn."

When they were alone Amedee gazed at Rosine sadly. She was pretty, in spite of her colorless complexion, a child of the faubourg, born with a genius for dress, who could clothe herself on nothing-a linen gown, a flower in her hat. One who lived on salads and vegetables, so as to buy well-made shoes and eighteen-button gloves.

The pretty blonde looked at Amedee, and a timid smile shone in her nut-brown eyes.

"Now, Monsieur Amedee," said she, at last, "it need not trouble you to meet at Bullier's the child whom you once played with. What would have been astonishing would be to find that I had become a fine lady. I am not wise, it is true, but I work, and you need not fear that I go with the first comer. Your friend is a handsome fellow, and very amiable, and I accepted his attentions because he knew Margot, while with you it is very different. It gives me pleasure to talk with you. It recalls Mamma Gerard, who was so kind to me. What has become of her, tell me? and her husband and her daughters?"

"Monsieur Gerard is dead," replied Amedee; "but the ladies are well, and I see them often."

"Do not tell them that you met me here, will you? It is better not. If I had had a good 'mother, like those girls, things would have turned out differently for me. But, you remember, papa was always interested in his politics. When I was fifteen years old he apprenticed me to a florist. He was a fine master, a perfect monster of a man, who ruined me! I say, Pere Combarieu has a droll trade now; he is manager of a Republican journal—nothing to do—only a few months in prison now and then. I am always working in flowers, and I have a little friend, a pupil at Val-de-Grace, but he has just left as a medical officer for Algeria. I was lonely all by myself, and this evening big Margot, whom I got acquainted with in the shop, brought me here to amuse myself. But you—what are you doing? Your friend said just now that you were a poet. Do you write songs? I always liked them. Do you remember when I used to play airs with one finger upon the Gerards' old piano? You were such a pretty little boy then, and as gentle as a girl. You still have your nice blue eyes, but they are a little darker. I remember them. No, you can not know how glad I am to see you again!"

They continued to chatter, bringing up old reminiscences, and when she spoke of the Gerard ladies she put on a respectful little air which pleased Amedee very much. She was a poor feather-headed little thing, he did not doubt; but she had kept at least the poor man's treasure, a simple heart. The young man was pleased with her prattling, and as he looked at the young girl he thought of the past and felt a sort of compassion for her. As she was silent for a moment, the poet said to her, "Do you know that you have become very pretty? What a charming complexion you have! such a lovely pallor!"

The grisette, who had known what poverty was, gave a bitter little laugh:

"Oh, my pallor! that is nothing! It is not the pallor of wealth."

Then, recovering her good-humor at once, she continued:

"Tell me, Monsieur Amedee, does this big Margot, whom you began to pay attentions to a little while ago, please you?"

Amedee quickly denied it. "That immense creature? Never! Now then, Rosine, I came here to amuse myself a little, I will admit. That is not forbidden at my age, is it? But this ball disgusts me. You have no appointment here? No? Is it truly no? Very well, take my arm and let us go. Do you live far from here?"

"In the Avenue d'Orleans, near the Montrouge church."

"Will you allow me to escort you home, then?"

She would be happy to, and they arose and left the ball. It seemed to the young poet as if the pretty girl's arm trembled a little in his; but once upon the boulevard, flooded by the light from the silvery moon, Rosine slackened her steps and became pensive, and her eyes were lowered when Amedee sought a glance from them in the obscurity. How sweet was this new desire that troubled the young man's heart! It was mixed with a little sentiment; his heart beat with emotion, and Rosine was not less moved. They could both find only insignificant things to say.

"What a beautiful night!"

"Yes! It does one good to breathe the fresh air."

They continued their walk without speaking. Oh, how fresh and sweet it was under these trees!

At last they reached the door of Rosine's dwelling. With a slow movement she pressed her hand upon the bell-button. Then Amedee, with a great effort, and in a confused, husky voice, asked whether he might go up with her and see her little room.

She looked at him steadily, with a tender sadness in her eyes, and then said to him, softly:

"No, certainly not! One must be sensible. I please you this evening, and you know very well that I think you are charming. It is true we knew each other when we were young, and now that we have met again, it seems as if it would be pleasant to love each other. But, believe me, we should commit a great folly, perhaps a wrong. It is better, I assure you, to forget that you ever met me at Bullier's with big Margot, and only remember your little playmate of the Rue Notre-Dame-des-Champs. It will be better than a caprice, it will be something pure that you can keep in your heart. Do not let us spoil the remembrance of our childhood, Monsieur Amedee, and let us part good friends."

Before the young man could find a reply, the bell pealed again, and Rosine gave Amedee a parting smile, lightly kissing the tips of her fingers, and disappeared behind the doer, which fell together, with a loud bang. The poet's first movements was one of rage. Giddy weather-cock of a woman! But he had hardly taken twenty steps upon the sidewalk before he said to himself, with a feeling of remorse, "She was right!" He thought that this poor girl had kept in one corner of her heart a shadow of reserve and modesty, and he was happy to feel rise within him a sacred respect for woman!

Amedee, my good fellow, you are quite worthless as a man of pleasure. You had better give it up!

CHAPTER XII

SOCIAL TRIUMPHS

For one month now Amedee Violette's volume of verses, entitled Poems from Nature, had embellished with its pale-blue covers the shelves of the book-shops. The commotion raised by the book's success, and the favorable criticisms given by the journals, had not yet calmed down at the Cafe de Seville.

This emotion, let it be understood, did not exist except among the literary men. The politicians disdained poets and poetry, and did not trouble them selves over such commonplace matters. They had affairs of a great deal more importance to determine the overthrow of the government first, then to remodel the map of Europe! What was necessary to over throw the Empire? First, conspiracy; second, barricades. Nothing was easier than to conspire. Every body conspired at the Seville. It is the character of the French, who are born cunning, but are light and talkative, to conspire in public places. As soon as one of our compatriots joins a secret society his first care is to go to his favorite restaurant and to confide, under a bond of the most absolute secrecy, to his most intimate friend, what he has known for about five minutes, the aim of the conspiracy, names of the actors, the day, hour, and place of the rendezvous, the passwords and countersigns. A little while after he has thus relieved himself, he is surprised that the police interfere and spoil an enterprise that has been prepared with so much mystery and discretion. It was in this way that the "beards" dealt in dark deeds of conspiracy at the Cafe de Seville. At the hour for absinthe and mazagran a certain number of Fiesques and Catilines were grouped around each table. At one of the tables in the foreground five old "beards," whitened by political crime, were planning an infernal machine; and in the back of the room ten robust hands had sworn upon the billiard-table to arm themselves for regicide; only, as with all "beards," there were necessarily some false ones among them, that is to say, spies. All the plots planned at the Seville had miserably miscarried.

The art of building barricades was also—you never would suspect it!—very ardently and conscientiously studied. This special branch of the science of fortification reckoned more than one Vauban and Gribeauval among its numbers. "Professor of barricading," was a title honored at the Cafe de Seville, and one that they would willingly have had engraved upon their visiting-cards. Observe that the instruction was only theoretical; doubtless out of respect for the policemen, they could not give entirely practical lessons to the future rioters who formed the ground-work of the business. The master or doctor of civil war could not go out with them, for instance, and practise in the Rue Drouot. But he had one resource, one way of getting out of it; namely, dominoes. No! you never would believe what a revolutionary appearance these inoffensive mutton-bones took on under the seditious hands of the habitues of the Cafe de Seville. These miniature pavements simulated upon the marble table the subjugation of the most complicated of barricades, with all sorts of bastions, redans, and counterscarps. It was something after the fashion of the small models of war-ships that one sees in marine museums. Any one, not in the secret, would have supposed that the "beards" simply played dominoes. Not at all! They were pursuing a course of technical insurrection. When they roared at the top of their lungs "Five on all sides!" certain players seemed to order a general discharge, and they had a way of saying, "I can not!" which evidently expressed the despair of a combatant who has burned his last cartridge. A "beard" in glasses and a stovepipe hat, who had been refused in his youth at the Ecole Polytechnique, was frightful in the rapidity and mathematical precision with which he added up in three minutes his barricade of dominoes. When this man "blocked the six," you were transported in imagination to the Rue Transnonain, or to the Cloitre St. Merry. It was terrible!

As to foreign politics, or the remodelling of the map of Europe, it was, properly speaking, only sport and recreation to the "beards." It added interest to the game, that was all. Is it not agreeable, when you are preparing a discard, at the decisive moment, with one hundred at piquet, which gives you 'quinte' or 'quatorze', to deliver unhappy Poland; and when one has the satisfaction to score a king and take every trick, what does it cost to let the Russians enter Constantinople?

Nevertheless, some of the most solemn "beards" of the Cafe de Seville attached themselves to international questions, to the great problem of European equilibrium. One of the most profound of these diplomats—who probably had nothing to buy suspenders with, for his shirt always hung out between his waistcoat and trousers—was persuaded that an indemnity of two million francs would suffice to obtain from the Pope the transfer of Rome to the Italians; and another Metternich on a small scale assumed for his specialty the business of offering a serious affront to England and threatening her, if she did not listen to his advice, with a loss in a short time of her Indian Empire and other colonial possessions.

Thus the "beards," absorbed by such grave speculations, did not trouble themselves about the vanity called literature, and did not care a pin for Amedee Violette's book. Among the long-haired ones, however, we repeat, the emotion was great. They were furious, they were agitated, and bristled up; the first enthusiasm over Amedee Violette's verses could not be lasting and had been only a mere flash. The young man saw these Merovingians as they really were toward a man who succeeded, that is, severe almost to cruelty. What! the first edition of Poems from Nature was exhausted and Massif had another in press! What! the bourgeoisie, far from being "astonished" at this book, declared themselves delighted with it, bought it, read it, and perhaps had it rebound! They spoke favorably of it in all the bourgeois journals, that is to say, in those that had subscribers! Did they not say that Violette, incited by Jocquelet, was working at a grand comedy in verse, and that the Theatre-Francais had made very flattering offers to the poet? But then, if he pleased the bourgeoisie so much he was—oh, horror!—a bourgeois himself. That was obvious. How blind they had been not to see it sooner! When Amedee had read his verses not long since at Sillery's, by what aberration had they confounded this platitude with simplicity, this whining with sincere emotion, these stage tricks with art? Ah! you may rest assured, they never will be caught again!

As the poets' tables at the Cafe de Seville had been for some time transformed into beds of torture upon which Amedee Violette's poems were stretched out and racked every day from five to seven, the amiable Paul Sillery, with a jeering smile upon his lips, tried occasionally to cry pity for his friend's verses, given up to such ferocious executioners. But these literary murderers, ready to destroy a comrade's book, are more pitiless than the Inquisition. There were two inquisitors more relentless than the others; first, the little scrubby fellow who claimed for his share all the houris of a Mussulman's palace; another, the great elegist from the provinces. Truly, his heartaches must have made him gain flesh, for very soon he was obliged to let out the strap on his waistcoat.

Of course, when Amedee appeared, the conversation was immediately changed, and they began to talk of insignificant things that they had read in the journals; for example, the fire-damp, which had killed twenty-five working-men in a mine, in a department of the north; or of the shipwreck of a transatlantic steamer in which everything was lost, with one hundred and fifty passengers and forty sailors—events of no importance, we must admit, if one compares them to the recent discovery made by the poet inquisitors of two incorrect phrases and five weak rhymes in their comrade's work.

Amedee's sensitive nature soon remarked the secret hostility of which he was the object in this group of poets, and he now came to the Cafe de Seville only on rare occasions, in order to take Paul Sillery by the hand, who, in spite of his ironical air, had always shown himself a good and faithful friend.

It was there that he recognized one evening his classmate of the Lycee, Arthur Papillon, seated at one of the political tables. The poet wondered to himself how this fine lawyer, with his temperate opinions, happened to be among these hot-headed revolutionists, and what interest in common could unite this correct pair of blond whiskers to the uncultivated, bushy ones. Papillon, as soon as he saw Amedee, took leave of the group with whom he was talking and came and offered his hearty congratulations to the author of Poems from Nature, leading him out upon the boulevard and giving him the key to the mystery.

All the old parties were united against the Empire, in view of the coming elections; Orleanists and Republicans were, for the time being, close friends. He, Papillon, had just taken his degree, and had attached himself to the fortunes of an old wreck of the July government; who, having rested in oblivion since 1852, had consented to run as candidate for the Liberal opposition in Seine-et-Oise. Papillon was flying around like a hen with her head cut off, to make his companion win the day. He came to the Seville to assure himself of the neutral goodwill of the unreconciled journalists, and he was full of hope.

"Oh! my dear friend, how difficult it is to struggle against an official candidate! But our candidate is an astonishing man. He goes about all day upon the railroads in our department, unfolding his programme before the travelling countrymen and changing compartments at each station. What a stroke of genius! a perambulating public assembling. This idea came to him from seeing a harpist make the trip from Havre to Honfleur, playing 'Il Bacio' all the time. Ah, one must look alive! The prefect does not shrink from any way of fighting us. Did he not spread through one of our most Catholic cantons the report that we were Voltairians, enemies to religion and devourers of priests? Fortunately, we have yet four Sundays before us, from now until the voting-day, and the patron will go to high mass and communion in our four more important parishes. That will be a response! If such a man is not elected, universal suffrage is hopeless!"

Amedee was not at that time so disenchanted with political matters as he became later, and he asked himself with an uneasy feeling whether this model candidate, who was perhaps about to give himself sacrilgious indigestion, and who showed his profession of faith as a cutler shows his knives, was not simply a quack.

Arthur Papillon did not give him time to devote himself to such unpleasant reflections, but said to him, in a frank, protecting tone:

"And you, my boy, let us see, where do you stand? You have been very successful, have you not? The other evening at the house of Madame la Comtesse Fontaine, you know—the widow of one of Louis Philippe's ministers and daughter of Marshal Lefievre—Jocquelet recited your 'Sebastopol' with enormous success. What a voice that Jocquelet has! We have not his like at the Paris bar. Fortunate poet! I have seen your book lying about in the boudoir of more than one beautiful woman. Well, I hope that you will leave the Cafe de Seville and not linger with all these badly combed fellows. You must go into society; it is indispensable to a man of letters, and I will present you whenever you wish."

For the time being Amedee's ardor was a little dampened concerning the Bohemians with whom he enjoyed so short a favor, and who had also in many ways shocked his delicacy. He was not desirous to be called "thou" by Pere Lebuffle.

But to go into society! His education had been so modest! Should he know how to appear, how to conduct himself properly? He asked this of Papillon. Our poet was proud, he feared ridicule, and would not consent to play an inferior role anywhere; and then his success just then was entirely platonic. He was still very poor and lived in the Faubourg St.-Jacques. Massif ought to pay him in a few days five hundred francs for the second edition of his book; but what is a handful of napoleons?

"It is enough," said the advocate, who thought of his friend's dress. "It is all that is necessary to buy fine linen, and a well cut dress-coat, that is the essential thing. Good form consists, above all things, in keeping silent. With your fine and yielding nature you will become at once a gentleman; better still, you are not a bad-looking fellow; you have an interesting pallor. I am convinced that you will please. It is now the beginning of July, and Paris is almost empty, but Madame la Comtesse Fontaine does not go away until the vacations, as she is looking after her little son, who is finishing his studies at the Lycee Bonaparte. The Countess's drawing-rooms are open every evening until the end of the month, and one meets there all the chic people who are delayed in Paris, or who stop here between two journeys. Madame Fontaine is a very amiable and influential old lady; she has a fancy for writers when they are good company. Do not be silly, but go and order yourself some evening clothes. By presenting you there, my dear fellow, I assure you, perhaps in fifteen years, a seat in the Academy. It is agreed! Get ready for next week."

Attention! Amedee Violette is about to make his first appearance in society.

Although his concierge, who aided him to finish his toilette and saw him put on his white cravat, had just said to him, "What a love of a husband you would make!" the poet's heart beat rapidly when the carriage in which he was seated beside Arthur Papillon stopped before the steps of an old house in the Rue de Bellechasse, where Madame la Comtesse Fontaine lived.

In the vestibule he tried to imitate the advocate's bearing, which was full of authority; but quickly despaired of knowing how to swell out his starched shirt-front under the severe looks of four tall lackeys in silk stockings. Amedee was as much embarrassed as if he were presented naked before an examining board. But they doubtless found him "good for service," for the door opened into a brightly lighted drawing-room into which he followed Arthur Papillon, like a frail sloop towed in by an imposing three-master, and behold the timid Amedee presented in due form to the mistress of the house! She was a lady of elephantine proportions, in her sixtieth year, and wore a white camellia stuck in her rosewood-colored hair. Her face and arms were plastered with enough flour to make a plate of fritters; but for all that, she had a grand air and superb eyes, whose commanding glance was softened by so kindly a smile that Amedee was a trifle reassured.

She had much applauded M. Violette's beautiful verse, she said, that Jocquelet had recited at her house on the last Thursday of her season; and she had just read with the greatest pleasure his Poems from Nature. She thanked M. Papillon—who bows his head and lets his monocle fall—for having brought M. Violette. She was charmed to make his acquaintance.

Amedee was very much embarrassed to know what to reply to this commonplace compliment which was paid so gracefully. Fortunately he was spared this duty by the arrival of a very much dressed, tall, bony woman, toward whom the Countess darted off with astonishing vivacity, exclaiming, joyfully: "Madame la Marechale!" and Amedee, still following in the wake of his comrade, sailed along toward the corner of the drawing-room, and then cast anchor before a whole flotilla of black coats. Amedee's spirits began to revive, and he examined the place, so entirely new to him, where his growing reputation had admitted him.

It was a vast drawing-room after the First Empire style, hung and furnished in yellow satin, whose high white panels were decorated with trophies of antique weapons carved in wood and gilded. A dauber from the Ecole des Beaux-Arts would have branded with the epithet "sham" the armchairs and sofas ornamented with sphinx heads in bronze, as well as the massive green marble clock upon which stood, all in gold, a favorite court personage, clothed in a cap, sword, and fig-leaf, who seemed to be making love to a young person in a floating tunic, with her hair dressed exactly like that of the Empress Josephine. But the dauber would have been wrong, for this massive splendor was wanting neither in grandeur nor character. Two pictures only lighted up the cold walls; one, signed by Gros, was an equestrian portrait of the Marshal, Madame Fontaine's father, the old drummer of Pont de Lodi, one of the bravest of Napoleon's lieutenants. He was represented in full-dress uniform, with an enormous black-plumed hat, brandishing his blue velvet baton, sprinkled with golden bees, and under the rearing horse's legs one could see in the dim distance a grand battle in the snow, and mouths of burning cannons. The other picture, placed upon an easel and lighted by a lamp with a reflector, was one of Ingre's the 'chef-d'oeuvres'. It was the portrait of the mistress of the house at the age of eighteen, a portrait of which the Countess was now but an old and horrible caricature.

Arthur Papillon talked in a low voice with Amedee, explaining to him how Madame Fontaine's drawing-room was neutral ground, open to people of all parties. As daughter of a Marshal of the First Empire, the Countess preserved the highest regard for the people at the Tuileries, although she was the widow of Count Fontaine, who was one of the brood of Royer-Collard's conservatives, a parliamentarian ennobled by Louis-Philippe, twice a colleague of Guizot on the ministerial bench, who died of spite and suppressed ambition after '48 and the coup d'etat. Besides, the Countess's brother, the Duc d'Eylau, married, in 1829, one of the greatest heiresses in the Faubourg St. Germain; for his father, the Marshal, whose character did not equal his bravery, attached himself to every government, and carried his candle in the processions on Corpus Christi Day under Charles X, and had ended by being manager of the Invalides at the beginning of the July monarchy. Thanks to this fortunate combination of circumstances, one met several great lords, many Orleanists, a certain number of official persons, and even some republicans of high rank, in this liberal drawing-room, where the Countess, who was an admirable hostess, knew how to attract learned men, writers, artists, and celebrities of all kinds, as well as young and pretty women. As the season was late, the gathering this evening was not large. However, neglecting the unimportant gentlemen whose ancestors had perhaps been fabricated by Pere Issacar, Papillon pointed out to his friend a few celebrities. One, with the badge of the Legion of Honor upon his coat, which looked as if it had come from the stall of an old-clothes man, was Forgerol, the great geologist, the most grasping of scientific men; Forgerol, rich from his twenty fat sinecures, for whom one of his confreres composed this epitaph in advance: "Here lies Forgerol, in the only place he did not solicit."

That grand old man, with the venerable, shaky head, whose white, silky hair seemed to shed blessings and benedictions, was M. Dussant du Fosse, a philanthropist by profession, honorary president of all charitable works; senator, of course, since he was one of France's peers, and who in a few years after the

Prussians had left, and the battles were over, would sink into suspicious affairs and end in the police courts.

That old statesman, whose rough, gray hairs were like brushes for removing cobwebs, a pedant from head to foot, leaning in his favorite attitude against the mantel decorated only with flowers, by his mulish obstinacy contributed much to the fall of the last monarchy. He was respectfully listened to and called "dear master" by a republican orator, whose red-hot convictions began to ooze away, and who, soon after, as minister of the Liberal empire, did his best to hasten the government's downfall.

Although Amedee was of an age to respect these notabilities, whom Papillon pointed out to him with so much deference, they did not impress him so much as certain visitors who belonged to the world of art and letters. In considering them the young man was much surprised and a little saddened at the want of harmony that he discovered between the appearance of the men and the nature of their talents. The poet Leroy des Saules had the haughty attitude and the Apollo face corresponding to the noble and perfect beauty of his verses; but Edouard Durocher, the fashionable painter of the nineteenth century, was a large, common-looking man with a huge moustache, like that of a book agent; and Theophile de Sonis, the elegant story-writer, the worldly romancer, had a copper-colored nose, and his harsh beard was like that of a chief in a custom-house.

What attracted Amedee's attention, above all things, were the women—the fashionable women that he saw close by for the first time. Some of them were old, and horrified him. The jewels with which they were loaded made their fatigued looks, dark-ringed eyes, heavy profiles, thick flabby lips, like a dromedary's, still more distressing; and with their bare necks and arms—it was etiquette at Madame Fontaine's receptions—which allowed one to see through filmy lace their flabby flesh or bony skeletons, they were as ridiculous as an elegant cloak would be upon an old crone.

As he saw these decrepit, painted creatures, the young man felt the respect that he should have for the old leave him. He would look only at the young and beautiful women, those with graceful figures and triumphant smiles upon their lips, flowers in their hair, and diamonds upon their necks. All this bare flesh intimidated Amedee; for he had been brought up so privately and strictly that he was distressed enough to lower his eyes at the sight of so many arms, necks, and shoulders. He thought of Maria Gerard as she looked the other day, when he met her going to work in the Louvre, so pretty in her short high-necked dress, her magnificent hair flying out from her close bonnet, and her box of pastels in her hand. How much more he preferred this simple rose, concealed among thorns, to all these too full-blown peonies!

Soon the enormous and amiable Countess came to the poet and begged him, to his great confusion, to recite a few verses. He was forced to do it. It was his turn to lean upon the mantel. Fortunately it was a success for him; all the full-blown peonies, who did not understand much of his poetry, thought him a handsome man, with his blue eyes, and their ardent, melancholy glance; and they applauded him as much as they could without bursting their very tight gloves. They surrounded him and complimented him. Madame Fontaine presented him to the poet Leroy des Saules, who congratulated him with the right word, and invited him with a paternal air to come and see him. It would have been a very happy moment for Amedee, if one of the old maids with camel-like lips, whose stockings were probably as blue as her eyelids, had not monopolized him for a quarter of an hour, putting him through a sort of an examination on contemporary poets. At last the poet retired, after receiving a cup of tea and an invitation to dinner for the next Tuesday. Then he was once more seated in the carriage with Arthur Papillon, who gave him a slap on the thigh, exclaiming, joyfully:

"Well, you are launched!"

It was true; he was launched, and he will wear out more than one suit of evening clothes before he learns all that this action "going into society," which seems nothing at all at first, and which really is nothing, implies, to an industrious man and artist, of useless activity and lost time. He is launched! He has made a successful debut! A dinner in the city! At Madame Fontaine's dinner on the next Tuesday, some abominable wine and aged salmon was served to Amedee by a butler named Adolphe, who ought rather to have been called Exili or Castaing, and who, after fifteen years' service to the Countess, already owned two good paying houses in Paris. At the time, however, all went well, for Amedee had a good healthy stomach and could digest buttons from a uniform; but when all the Borgias, in black-silk stockings and white-silk gloves, who wish to become house-owners, have cooked their favorite dishes for him, and have practised only half a dozen winters, two or three times a week upon him, we shall know more as to his digestion. Still that dinner was enjoyable. Beginning with the suspicious salmon, the statesman with the brush-broom head, the one who had overthrown Louis-Philippe without suspecting it, started to explain how, if they had listened to his advice, this constitutional king's dynasty would yet be upon the throne; and at the moment when the wretched butler poured out his most poisonous wine, the old lady who looked like a dromedary with rings in its ears, made Amedee—her unfortunate neighbor—undergo a new oral examination upon the poets of the nineteenth century, and asked him what he thought of Lamartine's clamorous debts, and Victor Hugo's foolish pride, and Alfred de Musset's intemperate habits.

The worthy Amedee is launched! He will go and pay visits of indigestion; appear one day at Madame such a one's, and at the houses of several other "Madames." At first he will stay there a half-hour, the simpleton! until he sees that the cunning ones only come in and go out exactly as one does in a booth at a fair. He will see pass before him—but this time in corsages of velvet or satin-all the necks and shoulders of his acquaintances, those that he turned away from with disgust and those that made him blush. Each Madame this one, entering Madame that one's house, will seat herself upon the edge of a chair, and will always say the same inevitable thing, the only thing that can be or should be said that day; for example, "So the poor General is dead!" or "Have you heard the new piece at the Francais? It is not very strong, but it is well played!" "This will be delicious;" and Amedee will admire, above all things, Madame this one's play of countenance, when Madame G——tells her that Madame B——'s daughter is to marry Madame C——'s nephew. While she hardly knows these people, she will manifest as lively a joy as if they had announced the death of an old aunt, whose money she is waiting for to renew the furniture in her house. And, on the contrary, when Madame D—announces that Madame E——'s little son has the whooping-cough, at once, without transition, by a change of expression that would make the fortune of an actress, the lady of the house puts on an air of consternation, as if the cholera had broken out the night before in the Halles quarter.

Amedee is launched, I repeat it. He is still a little green and will become the dupe, for a long time, of all the shams, grimaces, acting, and false smiles, which cover so many artificial teeth. At first sight all is elegance, harmony, and delicacy. Since Amedee does not know that the Princess Krazinska's celebrated head of hair was cut from the heads of the Breton girls, how could he suspect that the austere defender of the clergy, M. Lemarguillier, had been gravely compromised in a love affair, and had thrown himself at the feet of the chief of police, exclaiming, "Do not ruin me!" When the king of society is announced, the young Duc de la Tour-Prends-Garde, whose one ancestor was at the battle of the bridge, and who is just now introducing a new style in trousers, Amedee could not suspect that the favorite amusement of this fashionable rake consisted in drinking in the morning upon an empty stomach, with his coachman, at a grog-shop on the corner. When the pretty Baroness des Nenuphars blushed up to her ears because someone spoke the word "tea-spoon" before her, and she considered it to be an unwarrantable indelicacy—nobody knows why—it is assuredly not our young friend who will suspect that, in order to pay the gambling debts of her third lover, this modest person had just sold secretly her family jewels.

Rest assured Amedee will lose all these illusions in time. The day will come when he will not take in earnest this grand comedy in white cravats. He will not have the bad taste to show his indignation. No! he will pity these unfortunate society people condemned to hypocrisy and falsehood. He will even excuse their whims and vices as he thinks of the frightful ennui that overwhelms them. Yes, he will understand how the unhappy Duc de la Tour-Prends-Garde, who is condemned to hear La Favorita seventeen times during the winter, may feel at times the need of a violent distraction, and go to drink white wine with his servant. Amedee will be full of indulgence, only one must pardon him for his plebeian heart and native uncouthness; for at the moment when he shall have fathomed the emptiness and vanity of this worldly farce, he will keep all of his sympathy for those who retain something like nature. He will esteem infinitely more the poorest of the workmen—a wood-sawyer or a bell-hanger—than a politician haranguing from the mantel, or an old literary dame who sparkles like a window in the Palais-Royal, and is tattooed like a Caribbean; he will prefer an old; wrinkled, village grand-dame in her white cap, who still hoes, although sixty years old, her little field of potatoes.

CHAPTER XIII

A SERPENT AT THE FIRESIDE

A little more than a year has passed. It is now the first days of October; and when the morning mist is dissipated, the sky is of so limpid a blue and the air so pure and fresh, that Amedee Violette is almost tempted to make a paper kite and fly it over the fortifications, as he did in his youth. But the age for that has passed; Amedee's real kite is more fragile than if it had been made of sticks and pieces of old paper pasted on one over another; it does not ascend very high yet, and the thread that sails it is not very strong. Amedee's kite is his growing reputation. He must work to sustain it; and always with the secret hope of making little Maria his wife. Amedee works. He is not so poor now, since he earns at the ministry two hundred francs a month, and from time to time publishes a prose story in journals where his copy is paid for. He has also left his garret in the Faubourg St.-Jacques and lives on the Ile St. Louis, in one room only, but large and bright, from whose window he can see, as he leans out, the coming and going of boats on the river and the sun as it sets behind Notre-Dame.

Amedee has been working mostly upon his drama, for the Comedie-Francaise this summer, and it is nearly done; it is a modern drama in verse, entitled L'Atelier. The action is very simple, like that of a tragedy, but he believes it is sympathetic and touching, and it ends in a popular way. Amedee thinks he has used for his dialogue familiar but nevertheless poetic lines, in which he has not feared to put in certain graphic words and energetic speeches from the mouths of working-people.

The grateful poet has destined the principal role for Jocquelet, who has made a successful debut in the 'Fourberies de Scapin', and who, since then, has won success after success. Jocquelet, like all comic actors, aspires to play also in drama. He can do so in reality, but under particular conditions; for in spite of his grotesque nose, he has strong and spirited qualities, and recites verses very well. He is to represent an old mechanic, in his friend's work, a sort of faubourg Nestor, and this type will accommodate itself very well to the not very aristocratic face of Jocquelet, who more and more proves his cleverness at "making-up." However, at first the actor was not satisfied with his part. He fondles the not well defined dream of all actors, he wishes, like all the others, the "leading part." They do not exactly know what they mean by it, but in their dreams is vaguely visible a wonderful Almanzor, who makes his first entrance in an open barouche drawn by four horses harnessed a la Daumont, and descends from it dressed in tight-fitting gray clothes, tasselled boots, and decorations. This personage is as attractive as Don Juan, brave as Murat, a poet like Shakespeare, and as charitable as St. Vincent de Paul. He should have, before the end of the first act, crushed with love by one single glance, the young leading actress; dispersed a dozen assassins with his sword; addressed to the stars—that is to say, the spectators in the upper gallery—a long speech of eighty or a hundred lines, and gathered up two lost children under the folds of his cloak.

A "fine leading part" should also, during the rest of the piece, accomplish a certain number of sublime acts, address the multitude from the top of a staircase, insult a powerful monarch to his face, dash into the midst of a conflagration—always in the long-topped boots. The ideal part would be for him to discover America, like Christopher Columbus; win pitched battles, like Bonaparte, or some other equally senseless thing; but the essential point is, never to leave the stage and to talk all the time—the work, in reality, should be a monologue in five acts.

This role of an old workman, offered to Jocquelet by Amedee, obtained only a grimace of displeasure from the actor. However, it ended by his being reconciled to the part, studying it, and, to use his own expression, "racking his brains over it," until one day he ran to Violette's, all excited, exclaiming:

"I have the right idea of my old man now! I will dress him in a tricot waistcoat with ragged sleeves and dirty blue overalls. He is an apprentice, is he not? A fellow with a beard! Very well! in the great scene where they tell him that his son is a thief and he defies the whole of the workmen, he struggles and his clothes are torn open, showing a hairy chest. I am not hairy, but I will make myself so—does that fill the bill? You will see the effect."

While reserving the right to dissuade Jocquelet from making himself up in this way, Amedee carried his manuscript to the director of the Theatre Francais, who asked a little time to look it over, and also promised the young poet that he would read it aloud to the committee.

Amedee is very anxious, although Maurice Roger, to whom he has read the piece, act by act, predicts an enthusiastic acceptance.

The handsome Maurice has been installed for more than a year in a studio on the Rue d'Assas and leads a jolly, free life there. Does he work? Sometimes; by fits and starts. And although he abandons his sketches at the first attack of idleness, there is a charm about these sketches, suspended upon the wall; and he will some day show his talent. One of his greatest pleasures is to see pass before him all his beautiful models, at ten francs an hour. With palette in hand, he talks with the young women, tells them amusing stories, and makes them relate all their love-affairs. When friends come to see him, they can always see a model just disappearing behind a curtain. Amedee prefers to visit his friend on Sunday afternoons, and thus avoid meeting these models; and then, too, he meets there on that day Arthur Papillon, who paves the way for his political career by pleading lawsuits for the press. Although he is, at heart, only a very moderate Liberalist, this young man, with the very chic side whiskers, defends the most republican of "beards," if it can be called defending; for in spite of his fine oratorical efforts, his clients are regularly favored with the maximum of punishment. But they are all delighted with it, for the title of "political convict" is one very much in demand among the irreconcilables. They are all convinced that the time is near when they will overthrow the Empire, without suspecting, alas! that in order to do that twelve hundred thousand German bayonets will be necessary. The day after the triumph, the month of imprisonment will be taken into account, and St. Pelagie is not the 'carcere duro'. Papillon is cunning and wishes to have a finger in every pie, so he goes to dine once a week with those who owe their sojourn in this easy-going jail to him, and regularly carries them a lobster.

Paul Sillery, who has also made Maurice's acquaintance, loiters in this studio. The amiable Bohemian has not yet paid his bill to Pere Lebuffle, but he has cut his red fleece close to his head, and publishes every Sunday, in the journals, news full of grace and humor. Of course they will never pardon him at the Cafe de Seville; the "long-haired" ones have disowned this traitor who has gone over to the enemy, and is now only a sickening and fetid bourgeois; and if the poetical club were able to enforce its decrees, Paul Sillery, like an apostate Jew in the times of the Inquisition, would have been scourged and burned alive. Paul Sillery does not trouble himself about it, however; and from time to time returns to the "Seville" and treats its members to a bumper all around, which he pays for with the gold of his dishonor. Sometimes Jocquelet appears, with his smooth-shaved face; but only rarely, for he is at present a very busy man and already celebrated. His audacious nose is reproduced in all positions and displayed in photographers' windows, where he has for neighbors the negatives most in demand; for instance, the fatherly and benevolent face of the pope; Pius IX, or the international limbs of Mademoiselle Ketty, the majestic fairy, in tights. The journals, which print Jocquelet's name, treat him sympathetically and conspicuously, and are full of his praises. "He is good to his old aunt," "gives alms," "picked up a lost dog in the street the other evening." An artist such as he, who stamps immortality on all the comic repertory, and takes Moliere under his wing, has no time to go to visit friends, that is understood. However, he still honors Maurice Roger with short visits. He only has time to make all the knickknacks and china on the sideboard tremble with the noise of his terrible voice; only time to tell how, on the night before, in the greenroom, when still clothed in Scapin's striped cloak, he deigned to receive, with the coldest dignity, the compliments of a Royal Highness, or some other person of high rank. A prominent society lady has been dying of love for him the past six months; she occupies stage box Number Six—and then off he goes. Good riddance!

Amedee enjoys himself in his friend's studio, where gay and witty artists come to talk. They laugh and amuse themselves, and this Sunday resting-place is the most agreeable of the hard-working poet's recreations. Amedee prolongs them as long as possible, until at last he is alone with his friend; then the young men stretch themselves out upon the Turkish cushions, and they talk freely of their hopes, ambitions, and dreams for the future.

Amedee, however, keeps one secret to himself; he never has told of his love for Maria Gerard. Upon his return from Italy the traveller inquired several times for the Gerards, sympathized politely with their misfortune, and wished to be remembered to them through Amedee. The latter had been very reserved in his replies, and Maurice no longer broaches the subject in their conversation. Is it through neglect? After all, he hardly knew the ladies; still, Amedee is not sorry to talk of them no longer with his friend, and it is never without a little embarrassment and unacknowledged jealousy that he replies to Maria when she asks for news of Maurice.

She no longer inquires. The pretty Maria is cross and melancholy, for now they talk only of one thing at the Gerards; it is always the same, the vulgar and cruel thought, obtaining the means to live; and within a short time they have descended a few steps lower on the slippery ladder of poverty. It is not possible to earn enough to feed three mouths with a piano method and a box of pastels—or, at least, it does not hold out. Louise has fewer pupils, and Pere Issacar has lessened his orders. Mamma Gerard, who has become almost an old woman, redoubles her efforts; but they can no longer make both ends meet. Amedee sees it, and how it makes him suffer!

The poor women are proud, and complain as little as possible; but the decay inside this house, already so modest, is manifested in many ways. Two beautiful engravings, the last of their father's souvenirs, had been sold in an hour of extreme want; and one could see, by the clean spots upon the wall, where the frames once hung. Madame Gerard's and her daughters' mourning seemed to grow rusty, and at the Sunday dinner Amedee now brings, instead of a cake, a pastry pie, which sometimes constitutes the entire meal. There is only one bottle of old wine in the cellar, and they drink wine by the pot from the grocer's. Each new detail that proves his friends' distress troubles the sensitive Amedee. Once, having earned ten Louis from some literary work, he took the poor mother aside and forced her to accept one hundred francs. The unfortunate woman, trembling with emotion, while two large tears rolled down her cheeks, admitted that the night before, in order to pay the washerwoman, they had pawned the only clock in the house.

What can he do to assist them, to help them to lead a less terrible life? Ah! if Maria would have it so, they could be married at once, without any other expense than the white dress, as other poor people do; and they would all live together. He has his salary of twenty-four hundred francs, besides a thousand francs that he has earned in other ways. With Louise's lessons this little income would be almost sufficient. Then he would exert himself to sell his writings; he would work hard, and they could manage. Of course it would be quite an undertaking on his part to take all this family under his charge. Children might be born to them. Had he not begun to gain a reputation; had he not a future before him? His piece might be played and meet with success. This would be their salvation. Oh! the happy life that the four would lead together! Yes, if Maria could love him a little, if he persisted in hoping, if she had the courage, it was the only step to take.

Becoming enthusiastic upon this subject, Amedee decided to submit the question to the excellent Louise, in whom he had perfect confidence, and considered to be goodness and truth personified. Every Thursday, at six o'clock, she left a boarding-school in the Rue de la Rochechouart, where she gave lessons to young ladies in singing. He would go and wait for her as she came out that very evening. And there he met her. Poor Louise! her dress was lamentable; and what a sad countenance! What a tired, distressed look!

"What, you, Amedee!" said she, with a happy smile, as he met her.

"Yes, my dear Louise. Take my arm and let me accompany you part of the way. We will talk as we walk; I have something very serious to say to you, confidentially—important advice to ask of you."

The poet then began to make his confession. He recalled their childhood days in the Rue Notre-Dame-des-Champs, when they played together; it was as long ago as that that he had first begun to be charmed by little Maria. As soon as he became a young man he felt that he loved the dear child, and had always cherished the hope that he might inspire her with a tender sentiment and marry her some day. If he had not spoken sooner it was because he was too poor, but he had always loved her, he loved her now, and never should love any other woman. He then explained his plan of life in simple and touching terms; he would become Madame Gerard's son and his dear Louise's brother; the union of their two poverties would become almost comfort. Was it not very simple and reasonable? He was very sure that she would approve of it, and she was wisdom itself and the head of the family.

While he was talking Louise lowered her eyes and looked at her feet. He did not feel that she was trembling violently. Blind, blind Amedee! You do not see, you will never see, that she is the one who loves you! Without hope! she knows that very well; she is older than you, she is not pretty, and she will always be in your eyes an adopted elder sister, who once showed you your alphabet letters with the point of her knitting-needle. She has suspected for a long time your love for Maria; she suffers, but she is resigned to it, and she will help you, the brave girl! But this confession that you make, Maria's name that you murmur into her ear in such loving accents, this dream of happiness in which, in your artless egotism, you reserve for her the role of an old maid who will bring up your children, is cruel, oh! how cruel! They have reached the Boulevard Pigalle; the sun has set; the sky is clear and bright as a turquoise, and the sharp autumn wind detaches the last of the dried leaves from the trees. Amedee is silent, but his anxious glance solicits and waits for Louise's reply.

"Dear Amedee," said she, raising her frank, pure eyes to his face, "you have the most generous and best of hearts. I suspected that you loved Maria, and I would be glad to tell you at once that she loves you, so that we might hereafter be but one family—but frankly I can not. Although the dear child is a little frivolous, her woman's instinct must suspect your feeling for her, but she has never spoken of it to mamma or to me. Have confidence; I do not see anything that augurs ill for you in that. She is so young and so innocent that she might love you without suspecting it herself. It is very possible, probable even, that your avowal will enlighten her as to the state of her own heart. She will be touched by your love, I am sure, as well as by your devotion to the whole family. I hope, with all my heart, Amedee, that you will succeed; for, I can say it to you, some pleasure must happen in poor Maria's life soon. She has moments of the deepest sadness and attacks of weeping that have made me uneasy for some time. You must have noticed, too, that she is overwhelmed with ennui. I can see that she suffers more than mamma or I, at the hard life that we lead. It is not strange that she feels as she does, for she is pretty and attractive, and made for happiness; and to see the present and the future so sad! How hard it is! You can understand, my friend, how much I desire this marriage to take place. You are so good and noble, you will make Maria happy; but you have said it, I am the one who represents wisdom in our house. Let me have then a few days in which to observe Maria, to obtain her confidence, to discover perhaps a sentiment in her heart of which she is ignorant; and remember that you have a sure and faithful ally in me."

"Take your own time, dear Louise," replied the poet. "I leave everything to you. Whatever you do will be for the best."

He thanked her and they parted at the foot of the Rue Lepic. It was a bitter pleasure for the slighted one to give the young man her poor, deformed, pianist's hand, and to feel that he pressed it with hope and gratitude.

She desired and must urge this marriage. She said this over and over again to herself, as she walked up the steep street, where crowds of people were swarming at the end of their day's work. No! no! Maria did not care for Amedee. Louise was very sure of it; but at all events it was necessary that she should try to snatch her young sister from the discouragements and bad counsel of poverty. Amedee loved her and would know how to make her love him. In order to assure their happiness these two young people must be united. As to herself, what matter! If they had children she would accept in advance her duties as coddling aunt and old godmother. Provided, of course, that Maria would be guided, or, at least, that she would consent. She was so pretty that she was a trifle vain. She was nourishing, perhaps, nobody knew what fancy or vain hope, based upon her beauty and youth. Louise had grave fears. The poor girl, with her thin, bent shoulders wrapped up in an old black shawl, had already forgotten her own grief and only thought of the happiness of others, as she slowly dragged herself up Montmartre Hill. When she reached the butcher's shop in front of the mayor's office, she remembered a request of her mother's; and as is always the case with the poor, a trivial detail is mixed with the drama of life. Louise, without forgetting her thoughts, while sacrificing her own heart, went into the shop and picked out two breaded cutlets and had them done up in brown paper, for their evening's repast.

The day after his conversation with Louise, Amedee felt that distressing impatience that waiting causes nervous people. The day at the office seemed unending, and in order to escape solitude, at five o'clock he went to Maurice's studio, where he had not been for fifteen days. He found him alone, and the young artist also seemed preoccupied. While Amedee congratulated him upon a study placed upon an easel, Maurice walked up and down the room with his hands in his pocket, and eyes upon the floor, making no reply to his friend's compliments. Suddenly he stopped and looking at Amedee said:

"Have you seen the Gerard ladies during the past few days?"

Maurice had not spoken of these ladies for several months, and the poet was a trifle surprised.

"Yes," he replied. "Not later than yesterday I met Mademoiselle Louise."

"And," replied Maurice, in a hesitating manner, "were all the family well?"

"Yes."

"Ah!" said the artist, in a strange voice, and he resumed his silent promenade.

Amedee always had a slightly unpleasant sensation when Maurice spoke the name of the Gerards, but this time the suspicious look and singular tone of the young painter, as he inquired about them, made the poet feel genuinely uneasy. He was impressed, above all, by Maurice's simple exclamation, "Ah!" which seemed to him to be enigmatical and mysterious. But nonsense! all this was foolish; his friend's questions were perfectly natural.

"Shall we pass the evening together, my dear Maurice?"

"It is impossible this evening," replied Maurice, still continuing his walk. "A duty—I have an engagement."

Amedee had the feeling that he had come at an unfortunate time, and discreetly took his departure. Maurice had seemed indifferent and less cordial than usual.

"What is the matter with him?" said the poet to himself several times, while dining in the little restaurant in the Latin Quarter. He afterward went to the Comedie Francaise, to kill time, as well as to inquire after his drama of Jocquelet, who played that evening in 'Le Legataire Universel'.

The comedian received him in his dressing-room, being already arrayed in Crispin's long boots and black trousers. He was seated in his shirt-sleeves be fore his toilet-table, and had just pasted over his smooth lips the bristling moustache of this traditional personage. Without rising, or even saying "Good-day," he cried out to the poet as he recognized him in the mirror.

"No news as to your piece! The manager has not one moment to himself; we are getting ready for the revival of Camaraderie. But we shall be through with it in two days, and then—"

And immediately, talking to hear himself talk, and to exercise his terrible organ, he belched out, like the noise from an opened dam, a torrent of commonplace things. He praised Scribe's works, which they had put on the stage again; he announced that the famous Guillery, his senior in the comedy line, would be execrable in this performance, and would make a bungle of it. He complained of being worried to death by the pursuit of a great lady—"You know, stage box Number Six," and showed, with a conceited gesture, a letter, tossed in among the jars of paint and pomade, which smelled of musk. Then, ascending to subjects of a more elevated order, he scored the politics of the Tuileries, and scornfully exposed the imperial corruption while recognizing that this "poor Badingue," who, three days before, had paid a little compliment to the actor, was of more account than his surroundings.

The poet went home and retired, bewildered by such gossip. When he awoke, the agony of his thoughts about Maria had become still more painful.

When should he see Louise again? Would her reply be favorable? In spite of the fine autumn morning his heart was troubled, and he felt that he had no courage. His administrative work had never seemed more loathsome than on that day. His fellow-clerk, an amateur in hunting, had just had two days' absence, and inflicted upon him, in an unmerciful manner, his stories of slaughtered partridges, and dogs who pointed, so wonderfully well, and of course punctuated all this with numerous Pan-Pans! to imitate the report of a double-barrelled gun.

When he left the office Amedee regained his serenity a little; he returned home by the quays, hunting after old books and enjoying the pleasures of a beautiful evening, watching, in the golden sky, around the spires of Ste.-Chapelle, a large flock of swallows assembling for their approaching departure.

At nightfall, after dining, he resolved to baffle his impatience by working all the evening and retouching one act of his drama with which he was not perfectly content. He went to his room, lighted his lamp, and seated himself before his open manuscript. Now, then! to work! He had been silly ever since the night before. Why should he imagine that misfortune was in the air? Do such things as presentiments exist?

Suddenly, three light, but hasty and sharp knocks were struck upon his door. Amedee arose, took his lamp, and opened it. He jumped back—there stood Louise Gerard in her deep mourning!

"You?—At my rooms?—At this hour?—What has happened?"

She entered and dropped into the poet's armchair. While he put the lamp upon the table he noticed that the young girl was as white as wax. Then she seized his hands and pressing them with all her strength, she said, in a voice unlike her own—a voice hoarse with despair:

"Amedee, I come to you by instinct, as toward our only friend, as to a brother, as to the only man who will be able to help us repair the frightful misfortune which overwhelms us!" She stopped, stifled with emotion.

"A misfortune!" exclaimed the young man. "What misfortune? Maria?"

"Yes! Maria!"

"An accident?—An illness?"

Louise made a rapid gesture with her arm and head which signified: "If it were only that!" With her mouth distorted by a bitter smile and with lowered eyes, talking confusedly, she said:

"Monsieur Maurice Roger—yes—your friend Maurice! A miserable wretch!—he has deceived and ruined the unhappy child! Oh! what infamy!—and now—now—"

Her deathly pale face flushed and became purple to the roots of her hair.

"Now Maria will become a mother!"

At these words the poet gave a cry like some enraged beast; he reeled, and would have fallen had the table not been near. He sat down on the edge of it, supporting himself with his hands, completely frozen as if from a great chill. Louise, overcome with shame, sat in the armchair, hiding her face in her hands while great tears rolled down between the fingers of her ragged gloves.

A ROMANCE OF YOUTH

By FRANCOIS COPPEE

BOOK 4.

CHAPTER XIV

TOO LATE!

It had been more than three months since Maria and Maurice had met again. One day the young man went to the Louvre to see his favorite pictures of the painters of the Eighteenth Century. His attention was attracted by the beautiful hair of a young artist dressed in black, who was copying one of Rosalba's portraits. It was our pretty pastel artist whose wonderful locks disturbed all the daubers in the museum, and which made colorists out of Signol's pupils themselves. Maurice approached the copyist, and then both exclaimed at once:

"Mademoiselle Maria!"

"Monsieur Maurice!"

She had recognized him so quickly and with such a charming smile, she had not, then, forgotten him? When he used to visit Pere Gerard he had noticed that she was not displeased with him; but after such a long time, at first sight, to obtain such a greeting, such a delighted exclamation—it was flattering!

The young man standing by her easel, with his hat off, so graceful and elegant in his well-cut garments, began to talk with her. He spoke first, in becoming and proper terms, of her father's death; inquired for her mother and sister, congratulated himself upon having been recognized thus, and then yielding to his bold custom, he added:

"As to myself, I hesitated at first. You have grown still more beautiful in two years."

As she blushed, he continued, in a joking way, which excused his audacity:

"Amedee told me that you had become delicious, but now I hardly dare ask him for news of you. Ever since you have lived at Montmartre—and I know that he sees you every Sunday—he has never offered to take me with him to pay my respects. Upon my word of honor, Mademoiselle Maria, I believe that he is in love with you and as jealous as a Turk."

She protested against it, confused but still smiling.

Ah! if he had known of the dream that Maria had kept concealed in one corner of her heart ever since their first meeting. If he had known that her only desire was to be chosen and loved by this handsome Maurice, who had gone through their house and among poor Papa Gerard's bric-a-brac like a meteor! Why not, after all? Did she not possess that great power, beauty? Her father, her mother, and even her sister, the wise Louise, had often said so to her. Yes! from the very first she had been charmed by this young man with the golden moustache, and the ways of a young lord; she had hoped to please him, and later, in spite of poverty and death, she had continued to be intoxicated with this folly and to dream of this narcotic against grief, of the return of this Prince Charming. Poor Maria, so good and so artless, who had been told too many times that she was pretty! Poor little spoiled child!

When he left you yesterday, little Maria, after half an hour's pleasing conversation, Maurice said to you jokingly: "Do not tell Violette, above all, that we have met. I should lose my best friend." You not only said nothing to Amedee, but you told neither your mother nor your sister. For Louise and Madame Gerard are prudent and wise, and they would tell you to avoid this rash fellow who has accosted you in a public place, and has told you at once that you are beautiful and beloved. They would scold you; they would tell you that this young man is of a rich and distinguished family; that his mother has great ambitions for him; that you have only your old black dress and beautiful eyes, and to-morrow, when you return to the Louvre, Madame Gerard will establish herself near your easel and discourage the young gallant.

But, little Maria, you conceal it from your mother and Louise! You have a secret from your family! To-morrow when you make your toilette before the mirror and twist up your golden hair, your heart will beat with hope and vanity. In the Louvre your attention will be distracted from your work when you hear a man's step resound in a neighboring gallery, and when Maurice arrives you will doubtless be troubled, but very much surprised and not displeased, ah! only too much pleased. Little Maria, little Maria, he talks to you in a low tone now. His blond moustache is very near your cheek, and you do well to lower your eyes, for I see a gleam of pleasure under your long lashes. I do not hear what he says, nor your replies; but how fast he works, how he gains your confidence! You will compromise yourself, little Maria, if you keep him too long by your easel. Four o'clock will soon strike, and the watchman in the green coat, who is snoozing before Watteau's designs, will arouse from his torpor, stretch his arms, look at his watch, get up from his seat, and call out "Time to close." Why do you allow Maurice to help you arrange your things, to accompany you through the galleries, carrying your box of pastels? The long, lanky girl in the Salon Carre, who affects the English ways, the one who will never finish copying the "Vierge au coussin vert," has followed you into the Louvre court. Take care! She has noticed, envious creature, that you are very much moved as you take leave of your companion, and that you let your hand remain for a second in his! This old maid 'a l'anglaise' has a viper's tongue. To-morrow you will be the talk of the Louvre, and the gossip will spread to the 'Ecole des Beaux-Arts', even to Signol's studio, where the two daubers, your respectful admirers, who think of cutting their throats in your honor, will accost each other with a "Well, the pretty pastellist! Yes, I know, she has a lover."

If it was only a lover! But the pretty pastellist has been very careless, more foolish than the old maid or the two young fellows dream of. It is so sweet to hear him say: "I love you!" and so delicious to listen for the question: "And you, do you love me a little?" when she is dying to say, "Yes!" Bending her head and blushing with confusion under Maurice's ardent gaze, the pretty Maria ends by murmuring the fatal "Yes." Then she sees Maurice turn pale with joy, and he says to her, "I must talk to you alone; not before these bores." She replies: "But how? It is impossible!" Then he asks whether she does not trust him, whether she does not believe him to be an honest man, and the young girl's looks say more than any protestation would.

"Well! to-morrow morning at ten o'clock—instead of coming to the Louvre—will you? I will wait for you on the Quai d'Orsay, before the Saint-Cloud pier."

She was there at the appointed hour, overwhelmed with emotion and ready to faint. He took her by the arm and led her aboard the boat.

"Do you see, now we are almost alone. Give me the pleasure of wandering through the fields with you. It is such beautiful weather. Be tranquil, we shall return early."

Oh, the happy day! Maria sees pass before her, as she is seated beside Maurice, who is whispering in her ear loving words and whose glances cover her with caresses, as if in a dream, views of Paris that were not familiar to her, high walls, arches of bridges, then the bare suburbs, the smoking manufactories of Grenelle, the Bas Meudon, with its boats and public-houses. At last, on the borders of the stream, the park with its extensive verdure appeared.

They wandered there for a long time under the chestnut-trees, loaded with their fruit in its green shells. The sun, filtering through the foliage, dotted the walks with patches of light, and Maurice continued to repeat to Maria that he loved her; that he had never loved any one but her! that he had loved her from the very first time that he saw her at Pere Gerard's, and that neither time nor absence had been able to drive away the remembrance of her. And at this moment he imagined that it was true. He did not think that he was telling a lie. As to poor Maria, do not be too severe upon her! think of her youth, her poverty and imprisonment—she was overwhelmed with happiness. She could think of nothing to say, and, giving herself up into the young man's arms, she had hardly the strength to turn upon him, from time to time, her eyes tortured with love.

Is it necessary to tell how she succumbed? how they went to a restaurant and dined? Emotion, the heavy heat of the afternoon, champagne, that golden wine that she tasted for the first time, stunned the imprudent child. Her charming head slips down upon the sofa-pillow, she is nearly fainting.

"You are too warm," said Maurice. "This bright light makes you ill."

He draws the curtains; they are in the darkness, and he takes the young girl in his arms, covering her hands, eyes, and lips with kisses.

Doubtless he swears to her that she shall be his wife. He asks only a little time, a few weeks, in which to prepare his mother, the ambitious Madame Roger, for his unexpected marriage. Maria never doubts him, but overcome by her fault, she feels an intense shame, and buries her face on her lover's shoulder. She thinks then, the guilty girl, of her past; of her innocence and poverty, of her humble but honest home; her dead father, her mother and sister—her two mothers, properly speaking—who yet call her "little one" and always consider her as a child, an infant in all its purity. She feels impressed with her sin, and wishes that she might die there at once.

Oh! I beg of you, be charitable to the poor, weak Maria, for she is young and she must suffer!

Maurice was not a rascal, after all; he was in earnest when he promised to marry her without delay. He even meant to admit all to his mother the next day; but when he saw her she never had appeared so imposing to him, with her gray hair under her widow's cap. He shivered as he thought of the tearful scenes, the reproaches and anger, and in his indolence he said to himself: "Upon my honor, I will do it later!" He loves Maria after his fashion. He is faithful to her, and when she steals away an hour from her work to come to see him, he is uneasy at the least delay. She is truly adorable, only Maurice does not like the unhappy look that she wears when she asks him, in a trembling voice: "Have you spoken to your mother?" He embraces her, reassures her. "Be easy. Leave me time to arrange it." The truth is, that now he begins to be perplexed at the idea of this marriage. It is his duty, he knows that very well; but he is not twenty three years old yet. There is no hurry. After all, is it duty? the little one yielded easily enough. Has he not the right to test her and wait a little? It is what his mother would advise him, he is certain. That is the only reasonable way to look at it.

Alas, egotists and cowards always have a reason for everything!

How dearly poor Maria's foolish step has cost her! How heavily such a secret weighs upon the child's heart! For a few moments of uneasy intoxication with this man, whom she already doubts and who sometimes makes her afraid, she must lie to her mother without blushing or lowering her eyes, and enter Maurice's house veiled and hiding like a thief. But that is nothing yet. After some time of this agonizing life her health is troubled. Quickly she goes to find Maurice! She arrives unexpectedly and finds him lying upon the sofa smoking a cigar. Without giving him time to rise, she throws herself into his arms, and, bursting into sobs, makes her terrible avowal. At first he only gives a start of angry astonishment, a harsh glance.

"Bah! you must be mistaken."

"I am sure of it, I tell you, I am sure of it!"

She has caught his angry glance and feels condemned in advance. However, he gives her a cold kiss, and it is with a great effort that she stammers:

"Maurice—you must—speak to your mother—"

He rises with an impatient gesture and Maria seats herself—her strength is leaving her—while he walks up and down the room.

"My poor Maria," he begins in a hesitating manner, "I dared not tell you, but my mother will not consent to our marriage—now, at least."

He lies! He has not spoken to his mother; she knows it. Ah! unhappy creature! he does not love her! and, discouraged, with a rumbling noise in her ears, she listens to Maurice as he speaks in his soft voice.

"Oh! be tranquil. I shall not abandon you, my poor child. If what you say is true-if you are sure of it, then the best thing that you can do, you see, is to leave your family and come and live with me. At first we will go away from Paris; you can be confined in the country. We can put the child out to nurse; they will take care of the little brat, of course. And later, perhaps, my mother will soften and will understand that we must marry. No, truly, the more I think of it, the more I believe that that is the best way to do. Yes! I know very well it will be hard to leave your home, but what can you do, my darling? You can write your mother a very affectionate letter."

And going to her he takes her, inert and heartbroken, into his arms, and tries to show himself loving.

"You are my wife, my dear little wife, I repeat it. Are you not glad, eh! that we can live together?"

This is what he proposes to do. He thinks to take her publicly to his house and to blazon her shame before the eyes of everybody! Maria feels that she is lost. She rises abruptly and says to him in the tone of a somnambulist: "That will do. We will talk of it again."

She goes away and returns to Montmartre at a crazy woman's pace, and finds her mother knitting and her sister ready to lay the table-yes! as if nothing at all was the matter. She takes their hands and falls at their feet!

Ah, poor women!

They had already been very much tried. The decay of this worthy family was lamentable; but in spite of all, yesterday even, they endured their fate with resignation. Yes! the economy, the degrading drudgery, the old, mended gowns—they accepted all this without a murmur. A noble sentiment sustained and gave them courage. All three—the old mother in a linen cap doing the cooking and the washing, the elder sister giving lessons at forty sous, and the little one working in pastels—were vaguely conscious of representing something very humble, but sacred and noble—a family without a blemish on their name. They felt that they moved in an atmosphere of esteem and respect. "Those ladies upon the first floor have so many accomplishments," say the neighbors. Their apartment—with its stained woodwork, its torn wall, paper, but where they were all united in work and drawn closer and closer to each other in love—had still the sweetness of a home; and upon their ragged mourning, their dilapidated furniture, the meagre meat soup at night, the pure light of honor gleamed and watched over them. Now, after this guilty child's avowal, all this was ended, lost forever! There was a blemish upon their life of duty and poverty, upon their irreproachable past, even upon the father's memory. Certainly the mother and elder sister excused the poor creature who sobbed under their kisses and begged their pardon. However, when they gazed at each other with red eyes and dry lips, they measured the fall of the family; they saw for the first time how frightful were their destitution and distress; they felt the unbearable feeling of shame glide into their hearts like a sinister and unexpected guest who, at the first glance, makes one understand that he has come to be master of the lodging. This was the secret, the overwhelming secret, which the distracted Louise Gerard revealed that evening to her only friend, Amedee Violette, acting thus by instinct, as a woman with too heavy a burden throws it to the ground, crying for help.

When she had ended her cruel confidence, to which the poet listened with his face buried in his hands, and he uncovered his face creased and furrowed by the sudden wrinkles of despair, Louise was frightened.

"How I have wounded him!" she thought. "How he loves Maria!"

But she saw shining in the young man's eyes a gloomy resolution.

"Very well, Louise," muttered he, between his teeth. "Do not tell me any more, I beg of you. I do not know where to find Maurice at this hour, but he will see me to-morrow morning, rest easy. If the evil is not repaired—and at once!"

He did not finish; his voice was stifled with grief and rage, and upon an almost imperious gesture to leave, Louise departed, overcome by her undertaking.

No, Maurice Roger was not a villain. After Maria's departure he felt ashamed and displeased with himself. A mother! poor little thing! Certainly he would take charge of her and the child; he would behave like a gentleman. But, to speak plainly, he did not now love her as much as he did. His vagabond nature was already tired of his love-affair. This one was watered too much by tears. Bah! he was usually lucky, and this troublesome affair would come out all right like the others. Truly, it was as bad an accident as if one had fallen into a hole and broken his leg. But then, who could tell? Chance and time arrange many things. The child might not live, perhaps; at any rate, it was perfectly natural that he should wait and see what happened.

The next morning the reckless Maurice—who had not slept badly—was tranquilly preparing his palette while awaiting his model, when he saw Amedee Violette enter his studio. At the first glance he saw that the poet knew all.

"Maurice," said Amedee, in a freezing tone, "I received a visit from Mademoiselle Louise Gerard last evening. She told me everything—all, do you understand me perfectly? I have come to learn whether I am mistaken regarding you—whether Maurice Roger is an honest man."

A flame darted from the young artist's eyes. Amedee, with his livid complexion and haggard from a sleepless night and tears, was pitiful to see. And then it was Amedee, little Amedee whom Maurice sincerely loved, for whom he had kept, ever since their college days, a sentiment, all the more precious that it flattered his vanity, the indulgent affection and protection of a superior.

"Oh! Grand, melodramatic words already!" said he, placing his palette upon the table. "Amedee, my dear boy, I do not recognize you, and if you have any explanation that you wish to ask of your old friend, it is not thus that you should do it. You have received, you tell me, Mademoiselle Gerard's confidence. I know you are devoted to those ladies. I understand your emotion and I think your intervention legitimate; but you see I speak calmly and in a friendly way. Calm yourself in your turn and do not forget that, in spite of your zeal for those ladies, I am the best and dearest companion of your youth. I am, I know, in one of the gravest situations of my life. Let us talk of it. Advise me; you have the right to do so; but not in that tone of voice—that angry, threatening tone which I pardon, but which hurts and makes me doubt, were it possible, your love for me."

"Ah! you know very well that I love you," replied the unhappy Amedee, "but why do you need my advice? You are frank enough to deny nothing. You admit that it is true, that you have seduced a young girl. Does not your conscience tell you what to do?"

"To marry her? That is my intention. But, Amedee, do you think of my mother? This marriage will distress her, destroy her fond hopes and ambitions. I hope to be able to gain her consent; only I must have time to turn myself. Later—very soon. I do not say—if the child lives."

This word, torn from Maurice by the cynicism which is in the heart of all egotists, made Amedee angry.

"Your mother!" exclaimed he. "Your mother is the widow of a French officer who died facing the enemy. She will understand it, I am sure, as a matter of honor and duty. Go and find her, tell her that you have ruined this unfortunate child. Your mother will advise you to marry her. She will command you to do it."

This argument was forcible and direct, and impressed Maurice; but his friend's violence irritated him.

"You go to work badly, Amedee, I repeat it," said he, raising his tone. "You have no right to prejudge my mother's opinion, and I receive no orders from anybody. After all, nothing authorizes you to do it; if it is because you were in love with Maria—"

A furious cry interrupted him. Amedee, with wild eyes and shaking his fists, walked toward Maurice, speaking in a cutting tone:

"Well, yes! I loved her," said he, "and I wished to make her my wife. You, who no longer love her, who took her out of caprice, as you have taken others, you have destroyed all of my dreams for the future. She preferred you, and, understand me, Maurice, I am too proud to complain, too just to hold spite against you. I am only here to prevent your committing an infamy. Upon my honor! If you repulse me, our friendship is destroyed forever, and I dare not think of what will happen between us, but it will be terrible! Alas! I am wrong, I do not talk to you as I ought. Maurice, there is time yet! Only listen to your heart, which I know is generous and good. You have wronged an innocent child and driven a poor and worthy family to despair. You can repair the evil you have caused. You wish to. You will! I beg of you, do it out of respect for yourself and the name you bear. Act like a brave man and a gentleman! Give this young girl—whose only wrong has been in loving you too much—give the mother of your child your name, your heart, your love. You will be happy with her and through her. Go! I shall not be jealous of your happiness, but only too glad to have found my friend, my loyal Maurice once more, and to be able still to love and admire him as heretofore."

Stirred by these warm words, and fatigued by the discussion and struggle, the painter reached out his hands to his friend, who pressed them in his. Suddenly he looked at Amedee and saw his eyes shining with tears, and, partly from sorrow, but more from want of will and from moral weakness, to end it he exclaimed:

"You are right, after all. We will arrange this matter without delay. What do you wish me to do?"

Ah, how Amedee bounded upon his neck!

"My good, my dear Maurice! Quickly dress yourself. Let us go to those ladies and embrace and console that dear child. Ah! I knew very well that you would understand me and that your heart was in the right place. How happy the poor women will be! Now then, my old friend, is it not good to do one's duty?"

Yes, Maurice found that it was good now; excited and carried away by his friend, he hurried toward the good action that was pointed out to him as he would to a pleasure-party, and while putting on his coat to go out, he said:

"After all, my mother can only approve, and since she always does as I wish, she will end by adoring my little Maria. It is all right; there is no way of resisting you, Violette. You are a good and persuasive Violette. Now, then, here I am, ready—a handkerchief—my hat. Off we go!"

They went out and took a cab which carried them toward Montmartre. The easy-going Maurice, reconciled to his future, sketched out his plan of life. Once married, he would work seriously. At first, immediately after the ceremony, he would leave with his wife to pass the winter in the South, where she could be confined. He knew a pretty place in the Corniche, near Antibes, where he should not lose his time, as he could bring back marine and landscape sketches. But it would not be until the next winter that he would entirely arrange his life. The painter Laugeol was going to move; he would hire his apartment—"a superb studio, my dear fellow, with windows looking out upon the Luxembourg." He could see himself there now, working hard, having a successful picture in the Salon, wearing a medal. He chose even the hangings in the sleeping-rooms in advance. Then, upon beautiful days, how convenient the garden would be for the child and the nurse.

Suddenly, in the midst of this chattering, he noticed Amedee's sad face as he shrank into the back of the carriage.

"Forgive me, my dear friend," said he, taking him affectionately by the hand. "I forgot what you told me just now. Ah! fate is ridiculous, when I think that my happiness makes you feel badly."

The poet gave his friend a long, sad look.

"Be happy with Maria and make her happy, that is all I ask for you both."

They had reached the foot of Montmartre, and the carriage went slowly up the steep streets.

"My friend," said Amedee, "we shall arrive there soon. You will go in alone to see these ladies, will you not? Oh! do not be afraid. I know Louise and the mother. They will not utter one word of reproach. Your upright act will be appreciated by them as it merits—but you will excuse me from going with you, do you see? It would be too painful for me."

"Yes, I understand, my poor Amedee. As it pleases you. Now then, courage, you will be cured of it. Everything is alleviated in time," replied Maurice, who supposed everybody to have his fickle nature. "I shall always remember the service that you have rendered me, for I blush now as I think of it. Yes, I was going to do a villainous act. Amedee, embrace me."

They threw their arms about each other's neck, and the carriage stopped. Once on the sidewalk, Amedee noticed his friend's wry face as he saw the home of the Gerards, a miserable, commonplace lodging-house, whose crackled plastered front made one think of the wrinkles on a poor man's face. On the right and on the left of the entrance-door were two shops, one a butcher's, the other a fruiterer's, exhaling their fetid odors. But Amedee paid no attention to the delicate Maurice's repugnance, saying:

"Do you see that little garden at the end of the walk? It is there. Au revoir."

They separated with a last grasp of the hand. The poet saw Maurice enter the dark alley, cross the narrow court and push the gate open into the garden, and then disappear among the mass of verdure. How many times Amedee had passed through there, moved at the thought that he was going to see Maria; and Maurice crossed this threshold for the first time in his life to take her away. He wanted her! He had himself given his beloved to another! He had begged, almost forced his rival, so to speak, to rob him of his dearest hope! What sorrow!

Amedee gave his address to the driver and entered the carriage again. A cold autumn rain had commenced to fall, and he was obliged to close the windows. As he was jolted harshly through the streets of Paris at a trot, the young poet, all of a shiver, saw carriages streaming with water, bespattered pedestrians under their umbrellas, a heavy gloom fall from the leaden sky; and Amedee, stupefied with grief, felt a strange sensation of emptiness, as if somebody had taken away his heart.

When he entered his room, the sight of his furniture, his engravings, his books on their shelves, and his table covered with its papers distressed him. His long evenings of study near this lamp, the long hours of thought over some difficult work, the austere and cheerless year that he had lived there, all had been dedicated to Maria. It was in order to obtain her some day, that he had labored so assiduously and obstinately! And now the frivolous and guilty child was doubtless weeping for joy in Maurice's arms, her husband to-morrow?

Seated before his table, with his head buried in his hands, Amedee sank into the depths of melancholy. His life seemed such a failure, his fate so disastrous, his future so gloomy, he felt so discouraged and lonely, that for the moment the courage to live deserted him. It seemed to him that an invisible hand touched him upon the shoulder with compassion, and he had at once a desire and a fear to turn around and look; for he knew very well that this hand was that of the dead. He did not fancy it under the hideous aspect of a skeleton, but as a calm, sad, but yet very sweet face which drew him against its breast with a mother's tenderness, and made him and his grief sleep—a sleep without dreams, profound and eternal. Suddenly he turned around and uttered a frightful cry. For a moment he thought he saw, extended at his feet, and still holding a razor in his hand, the dead body of his unhappy father, a horrible wound in his throat, and his thin gray hair in a pool of blood!

He was still trembling with this frightful hallucination when somebody knocked at his door. It was the concierge, who brought him two letters.

The first was stamped with the celebrated name:

"Comedie Francaise, 1680." The manager announced in the most gracious terms that he had read with the keenest pleasure his drama in verse, entitled L'Atelier, and he hoped that the reading committee would accept this work.

"Too late!" thought the young poet, as he tore open the other envelope.

This second letter bore the address of a Paris notary, and informed M. Amedee Violette that M. Isidore Gaufre had died without leaving a will, and that, as nephew of the defunct, he would receive a part of the estate, still difficult to appraise, but which would not be less than two hundred and fifty or three hundred thousand francs.

Success and fortune! Everything came at once! Amedee was at first overwhelmed with surprise; but with all these unhoped-for favors of fortune, which did not give him the power to repair his misfortune, the noble poet deeply realized that riches and glory were not equal to a great love or a beautiful dream, and, completely upset by the irony of his fate, he broke into a harsh burst of laughter.

CHAPTER XV

REPARATION

The late M. Violette was not mistaken when he supposed M. Gaufre capable of disinheriting his family in favor of his servant-mistress, but Berenice was wanting in patience. The rough beard and cap of an irresistible sergeant-major were the ruin of the girl. One Sunday, when M. Gaufre, as usual, recited vespers at St. Sulpice, he found that for the first time in his life he had forgotten his snuff-box. The holy offices were unbearable to this hypocritical person unless frequently broken by a good pinch of snuff. Instead of waiting for the final benediction and then going to take his usual walk, he left his church warden's stall and returned unexpectedly to the Rue Servandoni, where he surprised Berenice in a loving interview with her military friend. The old man's rage was pitiful to behold. He turned the Normandy beauty ignominiously out of doors, tore up the will he had made in her favor, and died some weeks after from indigestion, and left, in spite of himself, all his fortune to his natural heirs.

Amedee's drama had been accepted by the Comedie Francaise, but was not to be brought out until spring. The notary in charge of his uncle's estate had advanced him a few thousand francs, and, feeling sad and not having the courage to be present at the marriage of Maurice and Maria, the poet wished at least to enjoy, in a way, his new fortune and the independence that it gave him; so he resigned his position and left for a trip to Italy, in the hope of dissipating his grief.

Ah, never travel when the heart is troubled! You sleep with the echo of a dear name in your thoughts, and the half sleep of nights on a train is feverish and full of nightmares. Amedee suffered tortures from it. In the midst of the continual noise of the cars he thought he could hear sad voices crying loudly the name of a beloved lost one. Sometimes the tumult would become quiet for a little; brakes, springs, wheels, all parts of the furious cast-iron machine seemed to him tired of howling the deafening rhythmical gallop, and the vigorously rocked traveller could distinguish in the diminished uproar a strain of music, at first confused like a groan, then more distinct, but always the same cruel, haunting monotone—the fragment of a song that Maria once sang when they were both children. Suddenly a mournful and prolonged whistle would resound through the night. The express rushed madly into a tunnel. Under the sonorous roof, the frightful concert redoubled, exasperating him among all these metallic clamors; but Amedee still heard a distant sound like that of a blacksmith's hammer, and each heavy blow made his heart bound painfully.

Ah! never travel, and above all, never travel alone, if your heart is sad! How hostile and inhospitable the first sensation is that one feels then when entering an unknown city! Amedee was obliged to submit to the tiresome delay of looking after his baggage in a commonplace station; the hasty packing into an omnibus of tired-out travellers, darting glances of bad humor and suspicion; to the reception upon the hotel steps by the inevitable Swiss porter with his gold-banded cap, murdering all the European languages, greeting all the newcomers, and getting mixed in his "Yes, sir," "Ja, wohl," and "Si, signor." Amedee was an inexperienced tourist, who did not drag along with him a dozen trunks, and had not a rich and indolent air; so he was quickly despatched by the Swiss polyglot into a fourth-story room, which looked out into an open well, and was so gloomy that while he washed his hands he was afraid of falling ill and dying there without help. A notice written in four languages hung upon the wall, and, to add to his cheerfulness, it advised him to leave all his valuables at the office of the hotel—as if he had penetrated a forest infested with brigands. The rigid writing warned him still further that they looked upon him as a probable sharper, and that his bill would be presented every five days.

The tiresome life of railroads and table-d'hotes began for him.

He would be dragged about from city to city, like a bag of wheat or a cask of wine. He would dwell in pretentious and monumental hotels, where he would be numbered like a convict; he would meet the same carnivorous English family, with whom he might have made a tour of the world without exchanging one word; swallowing every day the tasteless soup, old fish, tough vegetables, and insipid wine which have an international reputation, so to speak. But above all, he was to have the horror, every evening upon going to his room, of passing through those uniform and desolate corridors, faintly lighted by gas, where before each door are pairs of cosmopolitan shoes—heavy alpine shoes, filthy German boots, the conjugal boots of my lord and my lady, which make one think, by their size, of the troglodyte giants—awaiting, with a fatigued air, their morning polish.

The imprudent Amedee was destined to all sorts of weariness, all sorts of deceptions, and all the homesickness of a solitary traveller. At the sight of the famous monuments and celebrated sites, which have become in some way looked upon as models for painters and material for literary development, Amedee felt that sensation of "already seen" which paralyzes the faculty of admiration. Dare we say it? The dome in Milan, that enormous quiver of white marble arrows, did not move him. He was indifferent to the sublime medley of bronze in the Baptistery in Florence; and the leaning tower at Pisa produced simply the effect of mystification. He walked miles through the museums and silent galleries, satiated with art and glutted with masterpieces. He was disgusted to find that he could not tolerate a dozen "Adorations of the Shepherds," or fourteen "Descents from the Cross," consecutively, even if they were signed with the most glorious names. The scenes of suffering and martyrdom, so many times repeated, were particularly distasteful to him; and he took a still greater dislike even to a certain monk, always represented on his knees in prayer with an axe sticking in his tonsure, than to the everlasting St. Sebastian pierced with arrows. His deadened and depraved attention discerned only the disagreeable and ugly side of a work of art. In the adorable artless originals he could see only childish and barbarous drawing, and he thought the old colorists' yolk-of-an-egg tone monotonous.

He wished to spur his sensations, to see something extraordinary. He travelled toward Venice, the noiseless city, the city without birds or verdure, toward that silent country of sky, marble, and water; but once there, the reality seemed inferior to his dream. He had not that shock of surprise and enthusiasm in the presence of St. Mark's and the Doges' palace which he had hoped for. He had read too many descriptions of all these wonders; seen too many more or less faithful pictures, and in his disenchantment he recalled a lamp-shade which once, in his own home, had excited his childish imagination—an ugly lampshade of blue pasteboard upon which was printed a nocturnal fete, the illuminations upon the ducal palace being represented by a row of pin-pricks.

Once more I repeat it, never travel alone, and above all, never go to Venice alone and without love! For young married people in their honeymoon, or a pair of lovers, the gondola is a floating boudoir, a nest upon the waters like a kingfisher's. But for one who is sad, and who stretches himself upon the sombre cushions of the bark, the gondola is a tomb.

Toward the last of January, Amedee suddenly returned to Paris. He would not be obliged to see Maurice or his young bride at once. They had been married one month and would remain in the South until the end of winter. He was recalled by the rehearsals of his drama. The notary who had charge of his affairs gave him twelve thousand pounds' income, a large competency, which enabled him to work for the pure and disinterested love of art, and without concessions to common people. The young poet furnished an elegant apartment in an old and beautiful house on the Quai d'Orsay, and sought out some of his old comrades—among others Paul Sillery, who now held a distinguished place in journalism and reappeared a little in society, becoming very quickly reconciled with life.

His first call was upon Madame Roger. He was very glad to see Maurice's mother; she was a little sad, but indulgent to Maurice, and resigned to her son's marriage, because she felt satisfied that he had acted like a man of honor. He also went at once to Montmartre to embrace Louise and Madame Gerard, who received him with great demonstrations. They were not so much embarrassed in money matters, for Maurice was very generous and had aided his wife's family. Louise gave lessons now for a proper remuneration, and Madame Gerard was able to refuse, with tears of gratitude, the poet's offer of assistance, who filially opened his purse to her. He dined as usual with his old friends, and they had tact enough not to say too much about the newly married ones; but there was one empty place at the table. He was once more seized with thoughts of the absent, and returned to his room that evening with an attack of the blues.

The rehearsal of his piece, which had just begun at the Comedie Francaise, the long sittings at the theatre, and the changes to be made from day to day, were a useful and powerful distraction for Amedee Violette's grief. L'Atelier, when played the first week in April, did not obtain more than a respectful greeting from the public; it was an indifferent success. This vulgar society, these simple, plain, sentiments, the sweetheart in a calico gown, the respectable old man in short frock and overalls, the sharp lines where here and there boldly rang out a slang word of the faubourg; above all, the scene representing a mill in full activity, with its grumbling workmen, its machines in motion, even the continual puffing of steam, all displeased the worldly people and shocked them. This was too abrupt a change from luxurious drawing-rooms, titled persons, aristocratic adulteresses, and declarations of love murmured to the heroine in full toilette by a lover leaning his elbow upon the piano, with all the airs and graces of a first-class dandy. However, Jocquelet, in the old artisan's role, was emphatic and exaggerated, and an ugly and commonplace debutante was an utter failure. The criticisms, generally routine in character, were not gracious, and the least surly ones condemned Amedee's attempt, qualifying it as an honorable effort. There were some slashes; one "long-haired" fellow from the Cafe de Seville failed in his criticism—the very one who once wrote a description of the violation of a tomb—to crush the author of L'Atelier in an ultra-classical article, wherein he protested against realism and called to witness all the silent, sculptured authors in the hall.

It was a singular thing, but Amedee was easily consoled over his failure. He did not have the necessary qualities to succeed in the theatrical line? Very well, he would give it up, that was all! It was not such a great misfortune, upon the whole, to abandon the most difficult art of all, but not the first; which did not allow a poet to act his own free liking. Amedee began to compose verses for himself—for his own gratification; to become intoxicated with his own rhymes and fancies; to gather with a sad pleasure the melancholy flowers that his trouble had caused to blossom in his heart.

Meanwhile summer arrived, and Maurice returned to Paris with his wife and a little boy, born at Nice, and Amedee must go to see them, although he knew in advance that the visit would make him unhappy.

The amateur painter was handsomer than ever. He was alone in his studio, wearing his same red jacket. He had decorated and even crammed the room full of luxurious and amusing knickknacks. The careless young man received his friend as if nothing had happened between them, and after their greetings and inquiries as to old friends, and the events that had happened since their last meeting, they lighted their cigarettes.

"Well, what have you done?" asked the poet. "You had great projects of work. Have you carried out your plans? Have you many sketches to show me?"

"Upon my word, no! Almost nothing. Do you know, when I was there I abandoned myself to living; I played the lizard in the sun. Happiness is very engrossing, and I have been foolishly happy."

Then placing his hand upon his friend's, who sat near him, he added:

"But I owe that happiness to you, my good Amedee."

Maurice said this carelessly, in order to satisfy his conscience. Did he remember, did he even suspect how unhappy the poet had been, and was now, on account of this happiness? A bell rang.

"Ah!" exclaimed the master of the house, joyfully.

"It is Maria returning with the baby from a walk in the gardens. This little citizen will be six weeks old to-morrow, and you must see what a handsome little fellow he is already."

Amedee felt stifled with emotion. He was about to see her again! To see her as a wife and a mother was quite different, of course.

She appeared, raising the portiere with one hand, while behind her appeared the white bonnet and rustic face of the nurse. No! she was not changed, but maternity, love, and a rich and easy life had expanded her beauty. She was dressed in a fresh and charming toilette. She blushed when she first recognized Amedee; and he felt with sadness that his presence could only awaken unpleasant recollections in the young woman's mind.

"Kiss each other, like old acquaintances," said the painter, laughing, with the air of a man who is loved and sure of himself.

But Amedee contented himself with kissing the tips of her glove, and the glance with which Maria thanked him for this reserve was one more torture for him to endure. She was grateful to him and gave him a kind smile.

"My mother and my sister," said she, graciously, "often have the pleasure of a visit from you, Monsieur Amedee. I hope that you will not make us jealous, but come often to see Maurice and me."

"Maurice and me!" How soft and tender her voice and eyes became as she said these simple words, "Maurice and me!" Ah, were they not one! How she loved him! How she loved him!

Then Amedee must admire the baby, who was now awake in his nurse's arms, aroused by his father's noisy gayety. The child opened his blue eyes, as serious as those of an old man's, and peeped out from the depth of lace, feebly squeezing the finger that the poet extended to him.

"What do you call him?" asked Amedee, troubled to find anything to say.

"Maurice, after his father," quickly responded Maria, who also put a mint of love into these words.

Amedee could endure no more. He made some pretext for withdrawing and went away, promising that he would see them again soon.

"I shall not go there very often!" he said to himself, as he descended the steps, furious with himself that he was obliged to hold back a sob.

He went there, however, and always suffered from it. He was the one who had made this marriage; he ought to rejoice that Maurice, softened by conjugal life and paternity, did not return to his recklessness of former days; but, on the contrary, the sight of this household, Maria's happy looks, the allusions that she sometimes made of gratitude to Amedee; above all Maurice's domineering way in his home, his way of speaking to his wife like an indulgent master to a slave delighted to obey, all displeased and unmanned him. He always left Maurice's displeased with himself, and irritated with the bad sentiments that he had in his heart; ashamed of loving another's wife, the wife of his old comrade; and keeping up all the same his friendship for Maurice, whom he was never able to see without a feeling of envy and secret bitterness.

He managed to lengthen the distance between his visits to the young pair, and to put another interest into his life. He was now a man of leisure, and his fortune allowed him to work when he liked and felt inspired. He returned to society and traversed the midst of miscellaneous parlors, greenrooms, and Bohemian society. He loitered about these places a great deal and lost his time, was interested by all the women, duped by his tender imagination; always expending too much sensibility in his fancies; taking his desires for love, and devoting himself to women.

The first of his loves was a beautiful Madame, whom he met in the Countess Fontaine's parlors. She was provided with a very old husband belonging to the political and financial world; a servant of several regimes, who having on many occasions feathered his own nest, made false statements of accounts, and betrayed his vows, his name could not be spoken in public assemblies without being preceded by the epithet of honorable. A man so seriously occupied in saving the Capitol, that is to say, in courageously sustaining the stronger, approving the majorities in all of their mean actions and thus increasing his own ground, sinecures, tips, stocks, and various other advantages, necessarily neglected his charming wife, and took very little notice of the ridicule that she inflicted upon him often, and to which he seemed predestined.

The fair lady—with a wax doll's beauty, not very young, confining herself to George Sand in literature, making three toilettes a day, and having a large account at the dentist's—singled out the young poet with a romantic head, and rapidly traversed with him the whole route through the country of Love. Thanks to modern progress, the voyage is now made by a through train. After passing the smaller stations, "blushing behind the fan," a "significant pressure of the hand," "appointment in a museum," etc., and halting at a station of very little importance called "scruples" (ten minutes' pause), Amedee reached the terminus of the line and was the most enviable of mortals. He became Madame's lapdog, the essential ornament in her drawing-room, figured at all the dinners, balls, and routs where she appeared, stifled his yawns at the back of her box at the Opera, and received the confidential mission of going to hunt for sweetmeats and chocolates in the foyer. His recompense consisted in metaphysical conversations and sentimental seances, in which he was not long in discovering that his heart was blinded by his emotions. At the end of a few months of this commonplace happiness, the rupture took place without any regrets on either side, and Amedee returned, without a pang, the love-tokens he had received, namely: a photograph, a package of letters in imitation of fashionable romances, written in long, angular handwriting, after the English style, upon very chic paper; and, we must not forget, a white glove which was a little yellowed from confinement in the casket, like the beautiful Madame herself.

A tall girl, with a body like a goddess, who earned three hundred francs a month by showing her costumes on the Vaudeville stage, and who gave one louis a day to her hairdresser, gave Amedee a new experience in love, more expensive, but much more amusing than the first. There were no more psychological subtleties or hazy consciences; but she had fine, strong limbs and the majestic carriage of a cardinal's mistress going through the Rue de Constance in heavy brocade garments, to see Jean Huss burned; and her voluptuous smile showed teeth made to devour patrimonies. Unfortunately, Mademoiselle Rose de Juin's—that was the young lady's theatrical name—charming head was full of the foolishness and vanity of a poor actress. Her attacks of rage when she read an article in the journals which cut her up, her nervous attacks and torrents of tears when they gave her parts with only fifteen lines in a new piece, had begun to annoy Amedee, when chance gave him a new rival in the person of Gradoux, an actor in the Varietes, the ugly clown whose chronic cold in the head and ugly face seemed for twenty years so delicious to the most refined public in the world. Relieved of a large number of bank-notes, Violette discreetly retired.

He next carried on a commonplace romance with a pretty little girl whose acquaintance he made one evening at a public fete. Louison was twenty years old, and earned her living at a famous florist's, and was as pink and fresh as an almond-bush in April. She had had only two lovers, gay fellows—an art student first—then a clerk in a novelty store, who had given her the not very aristocratic taste for boating. It was on the Marne, seated near Louison in a boat moored to the willows on the Ile d'Amour, that Amedee obtained his first kiss between two stanzas of a boating song, and this pretty creature, who never came to see him without bringing him a bouquet, charmed the poet. He remembered Beranger's charming verses, "I am of the people as well, my love!" felt that he loved, and was softened. In reality, he had turned this naive head. Louison became dreamy, asked for a lock of his hair, which she always carried with her in her 'porte-monnaie', went to get her fortune told to know whether the dark-complexioned young man, the knave of clubs, would be faithful to her for a long time. Amedee trusted this simple heart for some time, but at length he became tired of her vulgarities. She was really too talkative, not minding her h's and punctuating her discourse with "for certain" and "listen to me, then," calling Amedee "my little man," and eating vulgar dishes. One day she offered to kiss him, with a breath that smelled of garlic. She was the one who left him, from feminine pride, feeling that he no longer loved her, and he almost regretted her.

Thus his life passed; he worked a little and dreamed much. He went as rarely as possible to Maurice Roger's house. Maurice had decidedly turned out to be a good husband, and was fond of his home and playing with his little boy. Every time that Amedee saw Maria it meant several days of discouragement, sorrow, and impossibility of work.

"Well! well!" he would murmur, throwing down his pen, when the young woman's face would rise between his thoughts and his page; "I am incurable; I shall always love her."

In the summer of 1870 Amedee, being tired of Paris, thought of a new trip, and he was upon the point of going again, unfortunate fellow! to see the Swiss porters who speak all the languages in the world, and to view the melancholy boots in the hotel corridors, when the war broke out. The poet's passage through the midst of the revolutionary "beards" in the Cafe de Seville, and the parliamentary cravats in the Countess's drawing-room, had disgusted him forever with politics. He also was very suspicious of the Liberal ministers and all the different phases of the malady that was destroying the Second Empire. But Amedee was a good Frenchman. The assaults upon the frontiers, and the first battles lost, made a burning blush suffuse his face at the insult. When Paris was threatened he asked for arms, like the others, and although he had not a military spirit, he swore to do his duty, and his entire duty, too. One beautiful September morning he saw Trochu's gilded cap passing among the bayonets; four hundred thousand Parisians were there, like himself, full of good-will, who had taken up their guns with the resolve to die steadfast. Ah, the misery of defeat! All these brave men for five months could only fidget about the place and eat carcases. May the good God forgive the timid and the prattler! Alas! Poor old France! After so much glory! Poor France of Jeanne d'Arc and of Napoleon!

CHAPTER XVI

IN TIME OF WAR

The great siege lasted nearly three months. Upon the thirtieth of November they had fought a battle upon the banks of the Marne, then for twenty-four hours the fight had seemed to slacken, and there was a heavy snow-storm; but they maintained that the second of December would be decisive. That morning the battalion of the National Guard, of which Amedee Violette was one, went out for the first time, with the order simply to hold themselves in reserve in the third rank, by the fort's cannons, upon a hideous plain at the east of Paris.

Truly this National Guard did not make a bad appearance. They were a trifle awkward, perhaps, in their dark-blue hooded cloaks, with their tin-plate buttons, and armed with breech-loading rifles, and encumbered with canteens, basins, and pouches, all having an unprepared and too-new look. They all came from the best parts of the city, with accelerated steps and a loud beating of drums, and headed, if you please, by their major on horseback, a truss-maker, who had formerly been quartermaster of the third hussars. Certainly they only asked for service; it was not their fault, after all, if one had not confidence in them, and if they were not sent to the front as soon as they reached the fortifications. While crossing the drawbridge they had sung the Marseillaise like men ready to be shot down. What spoiled their martial appearance, perhaps, were their strong hunting-boots, their leather leggings, knit gloves, and long gaiters; lastly, that comfortable air of people who have brought with them a few dainties, such as a little bread with something eatable between, some tablets of chocolate, tobacco, and a phial filled with old rum. They had not gone two kilometres outside the ramparts, and were near the fort, where for the time being the artillery was silent, when a staff officer who was awaiting them upon an old hack of a horse, merely skin and bones, stopped them by a gesture of the hand, and said sharply to their major to take position on the left of the road, in an open field. They then stacked their arms there and broke ranks, and rested until further orders.

What a dismal place! Under a canopy of dull clouds, the earth bare with half-melted snow, with the low fort rising up before them as if in an attitude of defence, here and there groups of ruined houses, a mill whose tall chimney and walls had been half destroyed by shells, but where one still read, in large black letters, these words, "Soap-maker to the Nobility;" and through this desolated country was a long and muddy road which led over to where the battle field lay, and in the midst of which, presenting a symbol of death, lay the dead body of a horse.

In front of the National Guard, on the other side of the road, a battalion, which had been strongly put to the test the night before, were cooking. They had retreated as far as this to rest a little, and had spent all that night without shelter under the falling snow. Exhausted, bespattered, in rags, they were dolefully crouched around their meagre green-wood fires; the poor creatures were to be pitied. Underneath their misshapen caps they all showed yellow, wrinkled, and unshaven faces. The bitter, cold wind that swept over the plain made their thin shoulders, stooping from fatigue, shiver, and their shoulder-blades protruded under their faded capes. Some of them were wounded, too slightly to be sent away in the ambulance, and wore about their wrists and foreheads bands of bloody linen. When an officer passed with his head bent and a humiliated air, nobody saluted him. These men had suffered too much, and one could divine an angry and insolent despair in their gloomy looks, ready to burst out and tell of their injuries. They would have disgusted one if they had not excited one's pity. Alas, they were vanquished!

The Parisians were eager for news as to recent military operations, for they had only read in the morning papers—as they always did during this frightful siege—enigmatical despatches and bulletins purposely bristling with strategic expressions not comprehensible to the outsider. But all, or nearly all, had kept their patriotic hopes intact, or, to speak more plainly, their blind fanatical patriotism, and were certain against all reason of a definite victory; they walked along the road in little groups, and drew near the red pantaloons to talk a little.

"Well, it was a pretty hot affair on the thirtieth, wasn't it? Is it true that you had command of the Marne? You know what they say in Paris, my children? That Trochu knows something new, that he is going to make his way through the Prussian lines and join hands with the helping armies—in a word that we are going to strike the last blow."

At the sight of these spectres of soldiers, these unhappy men broken down with hunger and fatigue, the genteel National Guards, warmly clad and wrapped up for the winter, commenced to utter foolish speeches and big hopes which had been their daily food for several months: "Break the iron circle;" "not one inch, not a stone;" "war to the knife;" "one grand effort," etc. But the very best talkers were speedily discouraged by the shrugging of shoulders and ugly glances of the soldiers, that were like those of a snarling cur.

Meanwhile, a superb sergeant-major of the National Guard, newly equipped, a big, full-blooded fellow, with a red beard, the husband of a fashionable dressmaker, who every evening at the beer-house, after his sixth glass of beer would show, with matches, an infallible plan for blocking Paris and crushing the Prussian army like pepper, and was foolish enough to insist upon it.

"Now then, you, my good fellow," said he, addressing an insignificant corporal just about to eat his stew, as if he were questioning an old tactician or a man skilled like Turenne or Davoust; "do you see? you hit it in this affair of day before yesterday. Give us your opinion. Are the positions occupied by Ducrot as strong as they pretend? Is it victory for to-day?"

The corporal turned around suddenly; with a face the color of boxwood, and his blue eyes shining with rage and defiance, he cried in a hoarse voice:

"Go and see for yourselves, you stay-at-homes!"

Saddened and heart-broken at the demoralization of the soldiers, the National Guards withdrew.

"Behold the army which the Empire has left us!" said the dressmaker's husband, who was a fool.

Upon the road leading from Paris, pressing toward the cannon's mouth which was commencing to grumble again in the distance, a battalion of militia arrived, a disorderly troop. They were poor fellows from the departments in the west, all young, wearing in their caps the Brittany coat-of-arms, and whom suffering and privation had not yet entirely deprived of their good country complexions. They were less worn out than the other unfortunate fellows whose turn came too often, and did not feel the cold under their sheepskins, and still respected their officers, whom they knew personally, and were assured in case of accident of absolution given by one of their priests, who marched in the rear file of the first company, with his cassock tucked up and his Roman hat over his eyes. These country fellows walked briskly, a little helter-skelter, like their ancestors in the time of Stofflet and M. de la Rochejaquelin, but with a firm step and their muskets well placed upon their shoulders, by Ste. Anne! They looked like soldiers in earnest.

When they passed by the National Guard, the big blond waved his cap in the air, furiously shouting at the top of his lungs:

"Long live the Republic!"

But once more the fanatical patriot's enthusiasm fell flat. The Bretons were marching into danger partly from desire, but more from duty and discipline. At the very first shot these simple-minded creatures reach the supreme wisdom of loving one's country and losing one's life for it, if necessary, without interesting themselves in the varied mystifications one calls government. Four or five of the men, more or less astonished at the cry which greeted them, turned their placid, countrified faces toward the National Guard, and the battalion passed by.

The dressmaker's husband—he did nothing at his trade, for his wife adored him, and he spent at cafes all the money which she gave him—was extremely scandalized. During this time Amedee Violette was dreamily walking up and down before the stacks of guns. His warlike ardor of the first few days had dampened. He had seen and heard too many foolish things said and done since the beginning of this horrible siege; had taken part too many times in one of the most wretched spectacles in which a people can show vanity in adversity. He was heart broken to see his dear compatriots, his dear Parisians, redouble their boasting after each defeat and take their levity for heroism. If he admired the resignation of the poor women standing in line before the door of a butcher's shop, he was every day more sadly tormented by the bragging of his comrades, who thought themselves heroes when playing a game of corks. The official placards, the trash in the journals, inspired him with immense disgust, for they had never lied so boldly or flattered the people with so much low meanness. It was with a despairing heart and the certitude of final disaster that Amedee, needing a little sleep after the fatigue, wandered through Paris's obscure streets, barely lighted here and there by petroleum lamps, under the dark, opaque winter sky, where the echoes of the distant cannonading unceasingly growled like the barking of monstrous dogs.

What solitude! The poet had not one friend, not one comrade to whom he could confide his patriotic sorrows. Paul Sillery was serving in the army of the

Loire. Arthur Papillon, who had shown such boisterous enthusiasm on the fourth of September, had been nominated prefet in a Pyrenean department, and having looked over his previous studies, the former laureate of the university examinations spent much of his time therein, far from the firing, in making great speeches and haranguing from the top of the balconies, in which speeches the three hundred heroes of antiquity in a certain mountain-pass were a great deal too often mentioned. Amedee sometimes went to see Jocquelet in the theatres, where they gave benefit performances for the field hospitals or to contribute to the molding of a new cannon. The actor, wearing a short uniform and booted to the thighs, would recite with enormous success poems of the times in which enthusiasm and fine sentiments took the place of art and common sense. What can one say to a triumphant actor who takes himself for a second Tyrtee, and who after a second recall is convinced that he is going to save the country, and that Bismarck and old William had better look after their laurels.

As to Maurice Roger, at the beginning of the campaign he sent his mother, wife, and child into the country, and, wearing the double golden stripe of a lieutenant upon his militia jacket, he was now at the outposts near his father's old friend, Colonel Lantz.

Owing to a scarcity of officers, they had fished up the old Colonel from the depths of his engineer's office, and had torn him away from his squares and compasses. Poor old fellow! His souvenirs of activity went as far back as the Crimea and Sebastopol. Since that time he had not even seen a pickaxe glisten in the sun, and, behold, they asked this worthy man to return to the trench, and to powder his despatches with earth ploughed up by bombs, like Junot at Toulon in the fearless battery.

Well, he did not say "No," and after kissing his three portionless daughters on the forehead, he took his old uniform, half-eaten up by moths, from a drawer, shook the grains of pepper and camphor from it, and, with his slow, red-tapist step, went to make his excavators work as far as possible from the walls and close by the Prussians. I can tell you, the men of the auxiliary engineers and the gentlemen with the American-caps had not joked for some time over his African cape or his superannuated cap, which seemed to date from Pere Bugeaud. One day, when a German bomb burst among them, and they all fell to the ground excepting Colonel Lantz, who had not flinched. He tranquilly settled his glasses upon his nose and wiped off his splashed beard as coolly as he had, not long since, cleaned his India-ink brushes. Bless me! it gave you a lesson, gentlemen snobs, to sustain the honor of the special army, and taught you to respect the black velvet plastron and double red bands on the trousers. In spite of his appearance of absence of mind and deafness, the Colonel had just before heard murmured around him the words "old Lantz," and "old dolphin." Very well, gentlemen officers, you know now that the old army was composed of good material!

Maurice Roger was ordered from his battalion to Colonel Lantz, and did his duty like a true soldier's son, following his chief into the most perilous positions, and he no longer lowered his head or bent his shoulders at the whistling of a bomb. It was genuine military blood that flowed in his veins, and he did not fear death; but life in the open air, absence from his wife, the state of excitement produced by the war, and this eagerness for pleasure common to all those who risk their lives, had suddenly awakened his licentious temperament. When his service allowed him to do so, he would go into Paris and spend twenty-four hours there, profiting by it to have a champagne dinner at Brebant's or Voisin's, in company with some beautiful girl, and to eat the luxurious dishes of that time, such as beans, Gruyere cheese, and the great rarity which had been secretly raised for three months on the fifth floor, a leg of mutton.

One evening Amedee Violette was belated upon the boulevards, and saw coming out of a restaurant Maurice in full uniform, with one of the pretty comedienes from the Varietes leaning upon his arm. This meeting gave Amedee one heart-ache the more. It was for such a husband as this, then, that Maria, buried in some country place, was probably at this very time overwhelmed with fears about his safety. It was for this incorrigible rake that she had disdained her friend from childhood, and scorned the most delicate, faithful, and tender of lovers.

Finally, to kill time and to flee from solitude, Amedee went to the Cafe de Seville, but he only found a small group of his former acquaintances there. No more literary men, or almost none. The "long-haired" ones had to-day the "regulation cut," and wore divers head-gears, for the most of the scattered poets carried cartridge-boxes and guns; but some of the political "beards" had not renounced their old customs; the war and the fall of the Empire had been a triumph for them, and the fourth of September had opened every career for them. Twenty of these "beards" had been provided with prefectures; at least all, or nearly all, of them occupied public positions. There was one in the Government of National Defence, and three or four others, chosen from among the most rabid ones, were members of the Committee on Barricades; for, improbable as the thing may seem today, this commission existed and performed its duties, a commission according to all rules, with an organized office, a large china inkstand, stamped paper, verbal reports read and voted upon at the beginning of each meeting; and, around a table covered with green cloth, these professional instigators of the Cafe de Seville, these teachers of insurrection, generously gave the country the benefit of the practical experience that they had acquired in practising with the game of dominoes.

The "beards" remaining in Paris were busied with employments more or less considerable in the government, but did not do very much, the offices in which they worked for France's salvation usually closed at four o'clock, and they went as usual to take their appetizers at the Cafe de Seville. It was there that Amedee met them again, and mixed anew in their conversations, which now dwelt exclusively upon patriotic and military subjects. These "beards" who would none of them have been able to command "by the right flank" a platoon of artillery, had all at once been endowed by some magical power with the genius of strategy. Every evening, from five to seven, they fought a decisive battle upon each marble table, sustained by the artillery of the iced decanter which represented Mount Valerien, a glass of bitters, that is to say, Vinoy's brigade, feigned to attack a saucer representing the Montretout batteries; while the regular army and National Guard, symbolized by a glass of vermouth and absinthe, were coming in solid masses from the south, and marching straight into the heart of the enemy, the match-box.

There were scheming men among these "beards," and particularly terrible inventors, who all had an infallible way of destroying at a blow the Prussian army, and who accused General Trochu of treason, and of refusing their offers, giving as a reason the old prejudices of military laws among nations. One of these visionary people had formerly been physician to a somnambulist, and took from his pocket—with his tobacco and cigarette papers—a series of bottles labelled: cholera, yellow fever, typhus fever, smallpox, etc., and proposed as a very simple thing to go and spread these epidemics in all the German camps, by the aid of a navigable balloon, which he had just invented the night before upon going to bed. Amedee soon became tired of these braggarts and lunatics, and no longer went to the Cafe de Seville. He lived alone and shut himself up in his discouragement, and he had never perhaps had it weigh more heavily upon his shoulders than this morning of the second of December, the last day of the battle of Champigny, while he was sadly promenading before the stacked guns of his battalion.

The dark clouds, heavy with snow, were hurrying by, the tormenting rumble of the cannons, the muddy country, the crumbling buildings, and these vanquished soldiers shivering under their rags, all threw the poet into the most gloomy of reveries. Then humanity so many ages, centuries, perhaps, old, had only reached this point: Hatred, absurd war, fratricidal murder! Progress? Civilization? Mere words! No rest, no peaceful repose, either in fraternity or love! The primitive brute always reappears, the right of the stronger to hold in its clutches the pale cadaver of justice! What is the use of so many religions, philosophies, all the noble dreams, all the grand impulses of the thought toward the ideal and good? This horrible doctrine of the pessimists was true then! We are, then, like animals, eternally condemned to kill each other in order to live? If that is so, one might as well renounce life, and give up the ghost!

Meanwhile the cannonading now redoubled, and with its tragic grumbling was mingled the dry crackling sound of the musketry; beyond a wooded hillock, which restricted the view toward the southeast, a very thick white smoke spread over the horizon, mounting up into the gray sky. The fight had just been resumed there, and it was getting hot, for soon the ambulances and army-wagons drawn by artillery men began to pass. They were full of the wounded, whose plaintive moans were heard as they passed. They had crowded the least seriously wounded ones into the omnibus, which went at a foot pace, but the road had been broken up by the bad weather, and it was pitiful to behold these heads shaken as they passed over each rut. The sight of the dying extended upon bloody mattresses was still more lugubrious to see. The frightful procession of the slaughtered went slowly toward the city to the hospitals, but the carriages sometimes stopped, only a hundred steps from the position occupied by the

National Guards, before a house where a provisionary hospital had been established, and left their least transportable ones there. The morbid but powerful attraction that horrible sights exert over a man urged Amedee Violette to this spot. This house had been spared from bombardment and protected from pillage and fire by the Geneva flag; it was a small cottage which realized the dream of every shopkeeper after he has made his fortune. Nothing was lacking, not even the earthen lions at the steps, or the little garden with its glittering weather-vane, or the rock-work basin for goldfish. On warm days the past summer passers-by might have seen very often, under the green arbor, bourgeoisie in their shirt-sleeves and women in light dresses eating melons together. The poet's imagination fancied at once this picture of a Parisian's Sunday, when suddenly a young assistant appeared at an open window on the first floor, wiping his hands upon his blood-stained apron. He leaned out and called to a hospital attendant, that Amedee had not noticed before, who was cutting linen upon a table in the garden:

"Well, Vidal, you confounded dawdler," exclaimed he, impatiently, "are those bandages ready? Good God! are we to have them to-day or tomorrow?"

"Make room, if you please!" said at this moment a voice at Amedee's elbow, who stepped aside for two stretchers borne by four brothers of the Christian doctrine to pass. The poet gave a start and a cry of terror. He recognized in the two wounded men Maurice Roger and Colonel Lantz.

Wounded, both of them, yes! and mortally. Only one hour ago.

Affairs had turned out badly for us down there, then, on the borders of the Marne. They did a foolish thing to rest one day and give the enemy time to concentrate his forces; when they wished to renew the attack they dashed against vast numbers and formidable artillery. Two generals killed! So many brave men sacrificed! Now they beat a retreat once more and lose the ground. One of the chief generals, with lowered head and drooping shoulders, more from discouragement than fatigue, stood glass in hand, observing from a distance our lines, which were breaking.

"If we could fortify ourselves there at least," said he, pointing to an eminence which overlooked the river, "and establish a redoubt—in one night with a hundred picks it could be done. I do not believe that the enemy's fire could reach this position—it is a good one."

"We could go there and see, General," said some one, very quietly.

It was Pere Lantz, the "old dolphin," who was standing there with Maurice beside him and three or four of the auxiliary engineers; and, upon my word, in spite of his cap, which seemed to date from the time of Horace Vernet's "Smala," the poor man, with his glasses upon his nose, long cloak, and pepper colored beard, had no more prestige than a policeman in a public square, one of those old fellows who chase children off the grass, threatening them with their canes.

"When I say that the German artillery will not reach there," murmured the head general, "I am not sure of it. But you are right, Colonel. We must see. Send two of your men."

"With your permission, General," said Pere Lantz, "I will go myself." Maurice bravely added at once:

"Not without me, Colonel!"

"As you please," said the General, who had already pointed his glass upon another point of the battlefield.

Followed by the only son of his companion in arms in Africa and the Crimea, this office clerk and dauber in watercolors walked to the front as tranquilly as he would have gone to the minister's office with his umbrella under his arm. At the very moment when the two officers reached the plateau, a projectile from the Prussian batteries fell upon a chest and blew it up with a frightful uproar. The dead and wounded were heaped upon the ground. Pere Lantz saw the foot-soldiers fleeing, and the artillery men harnessing their wagons.

"What!" exclaimed he, rising up to his full height, "do they abandon the position?"

The Colonel's face was transfigured; opening wide his long cloak and showing his black velvet plastron upon which shone his commander's cross, he drew his sword, and, putting his cap upon the tip of it, bareheaded, with his gray hair floating in the wind, with open arms he threw himself before the runaways.

"Halt!" he commanded, in a thundering tone. "Turn about, wretches, turn about! You are here at a post of honor. Form again, my men! Gunners, to your places! Long life to France!"

Just then a new shell burst at the feet of the Colonel and of Maurice, and they both fell to the ground.

Amedee, staggering with emotion and a heart bursting with grief and fear, entered the hospital behind the two litters.

"Put them in the dining-room," said one of the brothers. "There is nobody there. The doctor will come immediately."

The young man with the bloody apron came in at once, and after a look at the wounded man he gave a despairing shake of the head, and, shrugging his shoulders, said:

"There is nothing to be done they will not last long."

In fact, the Colonel was dying. They had thrown an old woollen covering over him through which the hemorrhage showed itself by large stains of blood which were constantly increasing and penetrating the cloth. The wounded man seemed to be coming out of his faint; he half opened his eyes, and his lips moved.

The doctor, who had just come in, came up to the litter upon which the old officer was lying and leaned over him.

"Did you wish to say anything?" he asked.

The old Colonel, without moving his head, turned his sad gaze upon the surgeon, oh! so sad, and in a voice scarcely to be heard he murmured:

"Three daughters—to marry—without a dowry! Three—three—!"

Then he heaved a deep sigh, his blue eyes paled and became glassy. Colonel Lantz was dead.

Do not despair, old military France! You will always have these simple-hearted soldiers who are ready to sacrifice themselves for your flag, ready to serve you for a morsel of bread, and to die for you, bequeathing their widows and orphans to you! Do not despair, old France of the one hundred years' war and of '92!

The brothers, who wore upon their black robes the red Geneva cross, were kneeling around the body and praying in a low tone. The assistant surgeon noticed Amedee Violette for the first time, standing motionless in a corner of the room.

"What are you doing here?" he asked him, brusquely.

"I am this poor officer's friend," Amedee replied, pointing to Maurice.

"So be it! stay with him—if he asks for a drink you have the tea there upon the stove. You, gentlemen," added he, addressing the brothers, who arose after making the sign of the cross, "you will return to the battle-field, I suppose?"

They silently bowed their heads, the eldest of them closed the dead man's eyes. As they were all going out together, the assistant surgeon said to them, in a petulant tone of voice:

"Try to bring me some not quite so much used up."

Maurice Roger was about to die, too. His shirt was stained with blood, and a stream ran down from his forehead upon his blond moustache, but he was still beautiful in his marble-like pallor. Amedee carefully raised up one of the wounded man's arms and placed it upon the stretcher, keeping his friend's hand in his own. Maurice moved slightly at the touch, and ended by opening his eyes.

"Ah, how thirsty I am!" he groaned.

Amedee went to the stove and got the pot of tea, and leaned over to help the unfortunate man drink it. Maurice looked at him with surprise. He recognized Amedee.

"You, Amedee!—where am I, then?"

He attempted in vain to rise. His head dropped slightly to the left, and he saw, not two steps from him, the lifeless body of his old colonel, with eyes closed and features already calmed by the first moments of perfect repose.

"My Colonel!" said he. "Ah! I understand—I remember-! How they ran away—miserable cowards! But you, Amedee? Why are you here—?"

His friend could not restrain his tears, and Maurice murmured:

"Done for, am I not?"

"No, no!" exclaimed Amedee, with animation. "They are going to dress your wounds at once—They will come soon! Courage, my good Maurice! Courage!"

Suddenly the wounded man had a terrible chill; his teeth chattered, and he said again:

"I am thirsty!—something to drink, my friend!—give me something to drink!"

A few swallows of tea calmed him a little. He closed his eyes as if to rest, but a moment after he opened them, and, fixing them upon his friend's face, he said to him in a faint voice:

"You know—Maria, my wife—marry her—I confide them to you—she and my son—"

Then, doubtless tired out by the fatigue of having spoken these words, he seemed to collapse and sink down into the litter, which was saturated now with his blood. A moment later he began to pant for breath. Amedee knelt by his side, and tears fell upon his hands, while between the dying man's gasps he could hear in the distance, upon the battlefield, the uninterrupted rumbling of the cannon as it mowed down others.

CHAPTER XVII

"WHEN YOUTH, THE DREAM, DEPARTS"

The leaves are falling!

This October afternoon is deliciously serene, there is not a cloud in the grayish-blue sky, where the sun, which has shed a pure and steady light since morning, has begun majestically to decline, like a good king who has grown old after a long and prosperous reign. How soft the air is! How calm and fresh! This is certainly one of the most beautiful of autumn days. Below, in the valley, the river sparkles like liquid silver, and the trees which crown the hill-tops are of a lurid gold and copper color. The distant panorama of Paris is grand and charming, with all its noted edifices and the dome of the Invalides shining like gold outlined upon the horizon. As a loving and coquettish woman, who wishes to be regretted, gives at the moment of departure her most intoxicating smile to a friend, so the close of autumn had put on for one of her last days all her splendid charms.

But the leaves are falling!

Amedee Violette is walking alone in his garden at Meudon. It is his country home, where he has lived for eight years. A short time after the close of the war he married Maurice's widow. He is walking upon the terrace planted with lindens that are now more than half-despoiled of their leaves, admiring the beautiful picture and thinking.

He is celebrated, he has worked hard and has built up a reputation by good, sincere books, as a poet. Doubtless, some persons are still jealous of him, and he is often treated with injustice, but he is estimated by the dignity of his life, which his love of art fills entirely, and he occupies a superior position in literature. Although his resources are modest, they are sufficient to exempt him from anxieties of a trivial nature. Living far from society, in the close intimacy of those that he loves, he does not know the miseries of ambition and vanity. Amedee Violette should be happy.

His old friend, Paul Sillery, who breakfasted with him that morning in Meudon, is condemned to daily labor and the exhausting life of a journalist; and when he was seated in the carriage which took him back to Paris that morning, to forced labor, to the article to be knocked off for tomorrow, in the midst of the racket and chattering of an editor's office, beside an interrupted cigar laid upon the edge of a table, he heaved a deep sigh as he thought of Amedee.

Ah, this Violette was to be envied! With money, home, and a family, he was not obliged to disseminate his ideas right and left. He had leisure, and could stop when he was not in the spirit of writing; he could think before he wrote and do some good work. It was not astonishing, to be sure, that he produced veritable works of art when he is cheered by the atmosphere of affection. First, he adores his wife, that is easily seen, and he looks upon Maurice's little son as his own, the little fellow is so pretty and attractive with his long, light curls. Certainly, one can see that Madame Violette has a never-to-be-forgotten grief, but what a kind and grateful glance she gives her husband! Could anything be more touching than Louise Gerard, that excellent old maid, the life of the house, who has the knack of making pleasing order and elegant comfort reign in the house, while she surrounds her mother, the paralytic Grandmother Gerard, with every care? Truly, Amedee has arranged his life well. He loves and is loved: he has procured for mind and body valuable and certain customs. He is a wise and fortunate man.

While Paul Sillery, buried in the corner of a carriage, allowed himself to be almost carried away by jealousy of his friend, Amedee, detained by the charm of this beautiful day which is drawing to a close, walks with slow, lingering steps under the lindens on the terrace.

The leaves are falling around him!

A very slight breeze is rising, the blue sky is fading a little below; in the nearest Paris suburb the windows are shining in the oblique rays of the setting sun. It will soon be night, and upon this carpet of dead leaves, which crackle under the poet's tread, other leaves will fall. They fall rarely, slowly, but continually. The frost of the night before has blighted them all. Dried up and rusty, they barely hang to the trees, so that the slightest wind that passes over them gathers them one after another, detaching them from their branches; whirling an instant in the golden light, they at last rejoin, with a sad little sound, their withered sisters, who sprinkle the gravel walks. The leaves fall, the leaves fall!

Amedee Violette is filled with melancholy.

He ought to be happy. What can he reproach destiny with? Has he not the one he always desired for his wife? Is she not the sweetest and best of companions for him? Yes! but he knows very well that she consented to marry him in order to obey Maurice's last wish, he knows very well that Maria's heart is buried in the soldier's grave at Champigny. She has set apart a sanctuary within herself where burns, as a perpetual light, the remembrance of the adored dead, of the man to whom she gave herself without reserve, the father of her son, the hero who tore himself from her arms to shed his blood for his country.

Amedee may be certain of the gratitude and devotion of his wife, but he never will have her love, for Maurice, a posthumous rival, rises between them. Ah, this Maurice! He had loved Maria very little or not very faithfully! She should remember that he had first betrayed her, that but for Amedee he would have abandoned her and she never would have been his wife. If she knew that in Paris when she was far away he had deceived her! But she never would know anything of it, for Amedee has too much delicacy to hurt the memory of the dead, and he respects and even admires this fidelity of illusion and love in Maria. He suffers from it. The one to whom he has given his name, his heart, and his life, is inconsolable, and he must be resigned to it. Although remarried, she is a widow at the bottom of her heart, and it is in vain that she puts on bright attire, her eyes and her smile are in mourning forever.

How could she forget her Maurice when he is before her every day in her son, who is also named Maurice and whose bright, handsome face strikingly resembles his father's? Amedee feels a presentiment that in a few years this child will be another Maurice, with the same attractions and vices. The poet does not forget that his dying friend confided the orphan to him, and he endeavors to be kind and good to him and to bring him up well. He sometimes has a feeling of sorrow when he discovers the same instincts and traits in the child as in the man whom he had so dearly loved and who had made him such trouble; in spite of all, he can not feel the sentiments of a father for another's son. His own union has been sterile.

Poor Amedee! Yet he is envied! The little joy that he has is mingled with grief and sorrow, and he dares not confide it to the excellent Louise—who suspects it, however—whose old and secret attachment for him he surmises now, and who is the good genius of his household. Had he only realized it before! It might have been happiness, genuine happiness for him!

The leaves fall! the leaves fall!

After breakfast, while they were smoking their cigars and walking along beside the masses of dahlias, upon which the large golden spider had spun its silvery web, Amedee Violette and Paul Sillery had talked of times past and the comrades of their youth. It was not a very gay conversation, for since then there had been the war, the Commune. How many were dead! How many had disappeared! And, then, this retrospective review proves to one that one can be entirely deceived as to certain people, and that chance is master.

Such an one, whom they had once considered as a great prose writer, as the leader of a sect, and whose doctrines of art five or six faithful disciples spread while copying his waistcoats and even imitating his manner of speaking with closed teeth, is reduced to writing stories for obscene journals. "Chose," the fiery revolutionist, had obtained a good place; and the modest "Machin," a man hardly noticed in the clubs, had published two exquisite books, genuine works of art.

All of the "beards" and "long-haired" men had taken unexpected paths. But the politicians, above all, were astonishing in the variety of their destinies. Among the cafe's frequenters at the hour for absinthe one could count eight deputies, three ministers, two ambassadors, one treasurer, and thirty exiles at Noumea awaiting the long-expected amnesty. The most interesting, everything considered, is that imbecile, that old fanatic of a Dubief, the man that never drank anything but sweetened water; for he, at least, was shot on the barricades by the Versaillese soldiers.

One person of whom the very thought disgusted the two friends was that jumping-jack of an Arthur Papillon. Universal suffrage, with its accustomed intelligence, had not failed to elect this nonentity and bombastic fool, and to-day he flounders about like a fish out of water in the midst of this political cesspool. Having been enriched by a large dowry, he has been by turns deputy, secretary, vice-president, president, head of committees, under secretary of State, in one word, everything that it was possible to be. For the time being he rants against the clergy, and his wife, who is ugly, rich, and pious, has just put their little girl into the Oiseaux school. He has not yet become minister, but rest assured he will reach that in time. He is very vain, full of confidence in himself, not more honest than necessary, and very obtrusive. Unless in the meantime they decide to establish a rotation providing that all the deputies be ministers by turns, Arthur Papillon is the inevitable, necessary man mentioned. In such a case, this would be terrible, for his eloquence would flow in torrents, and he would be one of the most agitating of microbes in the parliamentary culture.

And Jocquelet? Ah! the two friends only need to speak his name to burst into peals of laughter, for the illustrious actor now fills the universe with his glory and ridiculousness. Jocquelet severed the chain some time ago which bound him to the Parisian theatres. Like the tricolored flag, he has made the tour of Europe several times; like the English standard, he has crossed every ocean. He is the modern Wandering Actor, and the capitals of the Old World and both Americas watch breathless with desire for him to deign to shower over them the manna of his monologues. At Chicago, they detached his locomotive, and he intended, at the sight of this homage proportioned to his merits, to become a naturalized American citizen. But they proposed a new tour for him in old Europe, and out of filial remembrance he consented to return once more among us. As usual, he gathered a cartload of gold and laurels. He was painfully surprised upon reaching Stockholm by water not to be greeted by the squadrons with volleys of artillery, as was once done in honor of a famous cantatrice. Let Diplomacy look sharp! Jocquelet is indifferent to the court of Sweden!

After Paul Sillery's departure Amedee turned over in his mind various other recollections of former days. He has been a trifle estranged from Madame Roger since his marriage to Maria, but he sometimes takes little Maurice to see her. She has sheltered and given each of Colonel Lantz's daughters a dowry. Pretty Rosine Combarieu's face rises up before him, his childhood's companion, whom he met at Bullier's and never has seen since. What has become of the poor little creature? Amedee almost hopes that she is dead. Ah, how sad these old memories are in the autumn, when the leaves are falling and the sun is setting!

It has set, it has plunged beneath the horizon, and suddenly all is dark. Over the darkened landscape in the vast pearl-colored sky spreads the melancholy chill which follows the farewell of day. The white smoke from the city has turned gray, the river is like a dulled mirror. A moment ago, in the sun's last rays, the dead leaves, as they fell, looked like a golden rain, now they seem a dark snow.

Where are all your illusions and hopes of other days, Amedee Violette? You think this evening of the rapid flight of years, of the snowy flakes of winter which are beginning to fall on your temples. You have the proof to-day of the impossibility of absolutely requited love in this world. You know that happiness, or what is called so, exists only by snatches and lasts only a moment, and how commonplace it often is and how sad the next day! You depend upon your art for consolation. Oppressed by the monotonous ennui of living, you ask for the forgetfulness that only the intoxication of poetry and dreams can give you. Alas! Poor sentimentalist, your youth is ended!

And still the leaves fall!

Lightning Source UK Ltd.
Milton Keynes UK
UKOW08f0655010517
300251UK00001B/244/P

9 781406 848649